Please return this book on or before the date shown above. To renew go to www.essex.gov.uk/libraries, ring 0845 603 7628 or go to any Essex library.

Essex County Council

D1429236

She wanted to devour him on the spot.

Years of celibacy and an ugly duckling complex had made her ripe for this moment. Alex Zaphirides wanted her. Alex Zaphirides, who could have anyone. It just didn't make sense.

'Are you sure this isn't an any-port-in-a-storm thing?'

He heard the genuine bewilderment in her voice. She sounded small and impossibly young in the big, dark night. 'Maybe because I can see beneath all that camouflage? Behind the big glasses, baggy clothes and white coat. You are a beautiful woman, Isobella Nolan.'

How many years had it been since she'd been told that? She'd heard it so often in her younger years she'd never really appreciated it. Until now. Alex Zaphirides thought she was beautiful.

Her hand was on his bare chest, resting near his shoulder, and he was warm and solid. And he wanted her. He thought she was beautiful. Was he spinning her some pretty lies? No. She believed him. She'd heard enough false platitudes during her modelling years to know sincerity when she heard it…

Amy Andrews has always loved writing, and still can't quite believe that she gets to do it for a living. Creating wonderful heroines and gorgeous heroes and telling their stories is an amazing way to pass the day. Sometimes they don't always act as she'd like them to—but then neither do her kids, so she's kind of used to it. Amy lives in the very beautiful Samford Valley, with her husband and aforementioned children, along with six brown chooks and two black dogs. She loves to hear from her readers. Drop her a line at www.amyandrews.com.au

Recent titles by the same author:

THE SINGLE DAD'S NEW-YEAR BRIDE*
DR ROMANO'S CHRISTMAS BABY*
TOP-NOTCH SURGEON, PREGNANT NURSE*
THE OUTBACK DOCTOR'S SURPRISE BRIDE

Brisbane General Hospital

GREEK DOCTOR, CINDERELLA BRIDE

BY
AMY ANDREWS

MILLS & BOON

First published in Great Britain 2009
Large Print edition 2009
Harlequin Mills & Boon Limited,
Eton House, 18-24 Paradise Road,
Richmond, Surrey TW9 1SR

© Amy Andrews 2009

ISBN: 978 0 263 20550 3

Set in Times Roman 16½ on 18½ pt.
17-1209-52759

Harlequin Mills & Boon policy is to use papers that are
natural, renewable and recyclable products and made
from wood grown in sustainable forests. The logging and
manufacturing process conform to the legal environmental
regulations of the country of origin.

Printed and bound in Great Britain
by CPI Antony Rowe, Chippenham, Wiltshire

GREEK DOCTOR, CINDERELLA BRIDE

For my father. For everything.

Praise for Amy Andrews's previous titles

CHAPTER ONE

ISOBELLA NOLAN peered through her microscope at the latest skin scraping they'd been sent. The envenomation had occurred a few days ago off Darwin. The nematocysts were definitely those belonging to *Chironex Fleckeri*, more commonly known as the box jellyfish, and she gave an involuntary shudder.

A phone started to ring, breaking her concentration. Most days she could block out the background noise of the lab and its twenty research assistants, completely absorbed in her work. But today she couldn't settle. Meeting the big boss for the first time since she'd begun working for Dr Alexander Zaphirides two years ago was going to be nerve-racking.

Not least because she had a massive crush on him. Or on his voice anyway.

Isobella looked up from her microscope, identifying the offending noise as belonging to laboratory director Reg Barry's phone. Her immediate boss wasn't at his station, and she scowled at the insistent pealing, pushing her glasses back up her nose as she snatched up her own phone and stabbed her finger at the flashing light indicating Reg's extension.

'Hello? Trop Med Research, this is Isobella.' She peered back through the scope as she rattled off the standard greeting.

'Oh? Isobella? I thought I dialled Reg's extension?'

Isobella pulled away abruptly from the eyepieces and gripped the phone hard as the gravelled tones of Dr Alexander Zaphirides' voice rasped along her nerve-endings, raising the hairs on her arms and instantly tightening her nipples. She shut her eyes, letting it wreak its usual havoc on her central nervous system. *God, the man had a voice you could drown in!*

It was just louder than a whisper, its pitch husky, with a slight roughness to it that came and went. He seemed to have as little control over the pitch changes as a teenage boy, but there was nothing juvenile about it. It was smoother, softer, sexier. Mature. The slightly discernible accent hinting at his Greek heritage added an illicit edge. It was blatantly sinful. It was a voice that Lucifer would covet.

'Isobella? Are you still there?'

His voice whispered its treachery into her ear and she gripped the phone harder as her whole body responded to the rasp of his words. There was endless speculation around the lab as to the origins of his husky voice, ranging from growths on his vocal cords to a tragic accident. She preferred to think it the result of a misspent youth. Screaming rock songs into microphones, smoking a pack a day, and drinking way too much bourbon.

'Isobella?'

The pitch was louder this time, more insistent, less indulgent, and she sat up straight, blinking at the shocking direction of her thoughts. 'Sorry, Dr Zaphirides... I was...' *What? Fantasising about you in tight jeans and an earring?* Isobella cleared her throat. 'Reg isn't at his desk at the moment.'

'Oh, right. Well, I was just ringing to say that my flight's been delayed. Airport's fogged in. Crazy Melbourne weather. I'm going to be later than I thought. Probably won't be landing in Brisbane till late this afternoon.'

'Er, right. Okay. I'll let him know.'

'Thanks. See you later, Isobella.'

Isobella shivered as the husky note in his voice lengthened the vowel at the end of her name and dragged it out deliciously. His silky promise brushed along her skin as if he'd reached through the phone and physically caressed her.

Stop it!

This was stupid. He was her boss. And it was dimwitted in the extreme to fantasise about the man who had hired her and could just as easily fire her. For God's sake, she was going to be meeting him for the first time in a few hours. The last thing she needed was to blush furiously the minute he opened his mouth. Or swoon into a puddle at his feet the second he purred *Isobellaaaaaaa.*

Which she just might, if his looks were anywhere near as impressive as his voice. His voice said *masculine.* Movie-star. *Just-come-down-from-Mount-Olympus-Greek-sex-god.* And according to gossip—which Isobella abhorred, but which was unfortunately rife in the cloistered environment of a lab—he was the original tall, dark and handsome. Gossip also said he was autocratic, intelligent, intensely private and didn't suffer fools gladly.

Good. She'd hate to be working for an easily distracted, *laissez-faire* pretty boy, content to appeal only to the lowest common denominator. The dermonecrosis project she was heading up was too important for that.

Way more important than his appearance. And if his reputation was anything to go by he would resent the hell out of being gossiped about as if he was a prime piece of meat at a market. She better than anyone knew how insulting it was to be judged on physical appearance. The man was utterly brilliant, owning a string of highly successful labs all involved in cutting edge research.

Her own project was a typical example. It was more exciting than anything she'd ever done in her life—including walking a catwalk in Paris. It was ground-breaking stuff. He could look like the Elephant Man as far as she was concerned, and it wouldn't matter.

She realised she was still holding the phone, and replaced it as if it had scorched her palm. She had a busy day and she would *not* spend it thinking about her mysterious boss and his too-sexy-to-be-real voice. She had the sample to catalogue, a literature review to begin, and the finishing touches to put to the presentation Reg was giving at the symposium he and Alex were attending at the end of the week. She had more than enough on her plate.

Things didn't go according to plan, however. It seemed everything this morning was conspiring against her to prevent her from doing her work. The computer system kept crashing, necessitating several reloads of lost data, and when she went through the symposium presentation, the slides were for some reason all jumbled. To cap it all, it took her ages to find online articles for the literature review she was undertaking.

And of course her mind kept wandering to the owner of that voice, and the fact she would be face to face with him by day's end. Thank God she lived far, far away from that voice. The voice that had talked in her ear two or three times a week for the last two years. The voice that, despite its faultlessly businesslike, asexual tone, was in her dreams most nights.

Her mood grew blacker as the morning progressed, and when everyone started to leave for lunch she was grateful for some peace and quiet. She liked it best when she was alone in the lab. In fact her favourite part of the day was when everyone had gone home and there was just her, her microscope, and the background hum of the electronic gadgets that surrounded her.

Her stomach grumbled loudly. She'd been too nervous to stomach breakfast this morning—a most unusual occurrence for her. Thanks to a blessed metabolism she was always hungry, and right now she was starving! She pulled a muesli bar from her bag and munched at it as she tapped away at her keyboard.

She wouldn't be missed in the staffroom as she rarely ate lunch with her colleagues. It wasn't that Isobella didn't like the people she worked with; it was more that she resented wasting time away from her microscope. She loved to eat, but food and other human necessities came a poor second to the project. She could eat just as easily on the job.

Plus, being an intensely private person, she preferred her own company. Yes, here in the tropical medicine lab they were a team, a unit, all working towards a common goal, but the self-directed nature of her work appealed to the loner in Isobella.

In a lot of ways the lab was her refuge—a place where she could hide behind her glasses and white coat without censure—and whilst she was forced to share it with others, it didn't mean she had to make her life an open book.

In fact Isobella had a reputation at the lab for discouraging any form of interaction that didn't directly involve the project. She was polite, but distant. She'd never fostered close relationships or socialised outside of work hours. She didn't indulge in gossip or innuendo. In short, she was invisible. Which suited her just fine.

Oh, she knew in the beginning there'd been speculation about her. No one had been able to pigeonhole her, and that had obviously been intriguing. She'd have to have been stupid not to have known that her colleagues had talked about her behind her back. And, having rebuffed some early advances from male colleagues, she didn't need her science degree to figure out that her sexuality had been called into question.

But she had steadfastly ignored it all, concentrating on her work, weathering the gossip with aplomb, and gaining a good deal of respect in the process. And eventually, through quiet indifference, she'd dropped right off their radar.

Hmph! If only they knew. She'd walked the catwalks of Paris and Milan from the age of fourteen—the bitchiest workplace in the world. She'd suffered far greater insults.

'Hello? Anyone home?'

Isobella felt the hairs on the back of her neck stand to attention as the gravelly enquiry from the work area wrapped itself around her body. *Alex?* She leaned to the side slightly, looking around the partition that hid her desk from view.

'Hello?'

That voice again. It was him. Alexander Zaphirides. And it seemed as if the rumours had been spot-on—even in profile the man redefined tall, dark and handsome. He was dressed in an impeccably tailored navy pin-striped suit, with a pale lemon shirt beneath, left open at the neck, and devoid of a tie.

He wasn't supposed to be here yet.

Her hand clutched at her throat in a familiar comforting gesture, then she grabbed the edge of her desk and forced herself to her feet, stepping into the lab proper on shaky legs. 'Ah, yes— sorry, Dr Zaphirides.'

Alex turned slightly towards the voice. 'Isobella?'

Oh, God! His voice was even sexier in the flesh. She nodded, walking towards him, her outstretched hand trembling slightly. 'I didn't think you were due in till later?' Isobella hoped her voice sounded normal, because to her own ears it sounded high, practically a squeak.

'The airline managed to get me on an earlier flight,' Alex replied, shaking the proffered hand as she drew near, quickly assessing her baggy white coat and huge glasses. *So this was Isobella Nolan?* 'We meet at last, Isobella.'

Alex bowed his head slightly, and Isobella was curiously charmed by the old-fashioned gesture. She swallowed, her mouth suddenly parched, and forced a polite smile to her lips, ignoring the warmth of the big hand enveloping hers. She felt a silly flutter in her stomach.

'Nice to meet you, Dr Zaphirides,' she murmured.

At five-eleven Isobella didn't usually have to look up too far, but Alex had a good few inches on her. She blinked as she took in his features, her gaze zooming in on the splendour of his face. The man looked as if he really had just descended from Mount Olympus. His face was a work of art. Nobel and statuesque, with two indentations bracketing the chiselled perfection of his mouth.

He could have sat for Rodin. He certainly could have modelled for *GQ*. The planes of his face were sublime, his bone structure magnificent. His square jaw was dusted with dark stubble and his head was crowned with dark, lush locks styled into just-got-out-of-bed tousled glory, completing his god-like stature.

Alex dropped his hand. 'I think it's about time you called me Alex.'

His husky request brushed along her nerve-endings as his gaze captured hers. She was forced to concede that his eyes were almost as compelling as his voice. They were blue—a surprise, given his bronze colouring. A blue like she'd never seen before.

No, that wasn't true. She *had* seen it before. On a photo shoot on the volcanic isle of Santorini in Greece. The exact blue of the Aegean had been difficult to label back then, but she knew she was seeing it replicated in the cerulean depths of Alex Zaphirides's gaze.

She nodded. 'Of course, Dr… I mean, Alex.'

He laughed at her stumble, a sexy rasping chuckle that deepened the indentations either side of his mouth into flirty dimples and flashed a glimpse of his perfect white teeth. She looked away, momentarily dazzled, her gaze drawn to the bob of his Adam's apple in the bronzed column of his throat.

His open-necked shirt afforded her an unrestricted view, and her eyes widened at the large, L-shaped surgical scar that bisected half of his neck and ran up towards his right ear. It was white and faded, but still a noticeable mark. No wonder his voice was so gravelly. He'd obviously done some serious damage at some stage. But how? Which rumour was true?

Below it, a smaller but much more livid scar marred the centre of his throat. It was only a centimetre or so long, but it was raised, almost keloid in nature. She knew what it was without even having to ask, for she had a matching one of her own. At some stage in his life he'd had a tracheostomy. Were the two scars related?

She raised her hand nervously to her own throat, grateful to feel the familiar comforting presence of material covering her own unsightly blemish. She marvelled at how at ease with them Alex had to be to show his scars off to the world. Sixteen years later, she still reviled the marks that had disfigured her. She couldn't imagine a time when she'd *ever* be at ease with them.

'Where is everyone?' Alex enquired.

'They're in the staffroom, having lunch,' Isobella said, conscious of the thrum of blood through her head.

'And you?'

She frowned. He was looking expectantly at her, but it seemed all her usual thought processes were scrambled by his sandpaper voice and the sexier-than-Zeus vibes he emitted. 'I'm sorry?'

'You don't eat lunch?' He looked her up and down. Beneath her primly buttoned, baggy white coat he could just make out a lanky frame, and despite the distraction of her hideous too-big-for-her-face glasses her dainty bone structure was clearly evident. His mother would cluck her tongue in disapproval.

Isobella blushed under his scrutiny. He was looking at her as if she was a particularly uninteresting lab specimen. A first for her. Most men needed to fall prey to her sharp tongue and experience her specialised freezing-out routine before they looked at her with such complete uninterest.

She shrugged. 'I usually just grab a bite at my desk. There's always so much to do.'

Alex frowned. Just last week Reg had mentioned Isobella's tendency to become completely absorbed in her work. Her dedication was impressive, but Isobella Nolan was a workplace health and safety nightmare. 'You do understand the importance of regular breaks? It's not good for you to be hunched over a microscope all day.'

Isobella blinked. She'd have thought Alexander Zaphirides would understand her drive. She'd bet good money he hadn't got to where he was today, a pin-up boy for medical enterprise, by strict adherence to the rules. 'Don't worry. I mix it up.'

Alex frowned again. He suspected from what Reg said that she didn't 'mix it up' as much as she should. 'Good. I can't afford to have one of my team leaders and best researchers off work because she isn't following guidelines. The project must always be paramount.'

The intenseness of his Aegean gaze as it burrowed into hers was intimidating, and she nodded dumbly as his husky compliment was completely obliterated by his gravelly reprimand of her work practices. 'Of course, Dr Zaphirides.' She saw his full lips flatten. 'I mean…Alex.'

He nodded. Her prim politeness bothered him for reasons he couldn't quite pinpoint. 'I'll catch up with you later.'

Isobella could only stare after him. His long-legged, narrow-hipped, broad-shouldered retreat was fascinating, despite the slow burn of pique rising in her chest. The last thing she saw as he disappeared was the decadent brush of his hair against his collar.

She almost sagged to the ground in relief when he left, and stumbled back to her desk, sitting down with shaking knees. The whole atmosphere had seemed charged by his enigmatic presence, and she was pleased to be alone as reaction to his sheer masculine beauty took over.

Well, the rumours weren't wrong. He was sexy and autocratic in spades, and his commanding Greek heritage gave him an edge—an extra dollop of authority that was impressive. Quite what he was doing locked away in a lab she wasn't sure. Alexander Zaphirides should be gracing magazine covers, selling aftershave and whisky and expensive watches.

And Isobella knew what she was talking about. At the zenith of her international career she'd worked with some of the world's top male models. She had no doubt that Alex could have moved easily amongst their number.

She groaned inwardly. Great! Not only did the

man have a voice that could practically bring her to orgasm over the phone, but he had a body that was giving her the vapours after only a few minutes in his company. What the hell was the matter with her? The man had wrapped a thinly veiled criticism in a compliment. Questioned her commitment to the project. No one did that.

How dare he?

Two hours later, Alex watched Isobella surreptitiously as she peered through her microscope. The dreadful large dark-rimmed glasses that marred her face butted against the eyepieces of the scope. Her long platinum-blonde fringe had flopped forward from its side parting, and instead of sweeping elegantly across her forehead, as it had earlier, it obscured her face from him.

Her hair was cropped severely at the back, almost boyish in its brevity, shaped into the contours of her skull, exposing cute ears and feathered lightly at her nape. He caught a hint of bare flesh before the high collar of her shirt encroached on the very elegant line of her neck.

She was *so* not what he'd imagined. Not that he'd spent his days and nights wondering what one research assistant in his Brisbane lab looked like, but it bugged him nonetheless. He was usually very good at mental imaging. He had spoken to Isobella on a regular basis for two years, and with her precise speech, her prim and proper vocabulary and her polite way of keeping things strictly business had pegged her as a mousy middle-aged spinster.

And she appeared to be working overtime trying to project that image. Except she was failing miserably. The glasses were a classic example. He'd definitely expected to see her wearing a pair—even a pair that most respectable grandmothers wouldn't be seen dead in—but somehow they didn't disguise her features.

Instead the large, ugly frames accentuated the kittenesque quality of her make-up-less face. Its heart-shaped perfection. The delicateness of her nose, with its fascinating tilt at the tip. The mastery of her high cheekbones.

Nor did the two-sizes-too-big white lab coat hide anything. It hung on her like a sack, only emphasising the slightness beneath. The shapeless covering hinted at the litheness of her frame in all its small-boned glory. The pertness of her breasts and the flatness of her stomach. It was more alluring in a lot of ways than a skintight outfit would have been. It teased, hinted, heightened.

The same could be said for the baggy tracksuit pants she wore. Every movement, every twist and pivot as she reached for equipment, outlined the narrowness of her calves beneath. Her height worked against her, and a glimpse of slim ankle peeked out between the hem and the sock line of her very sensible, workplace-health-and-safety-approved closed-in shoes.

She twiddled the knob on her microscope and his gaze was drawn to her long, elegant fingers. They were free of jewellery, and he tried hard to think if he knew *any* female over the age of twelve who didn't wear at least one ring. Her nails were cut short and polish-free. Everything about her said plain, ordinary. It said, *Don't look at me, pass me by, ignore me.* So why was he so compelled to notice?

Because. Because despite her efforts to the contrary she was classically beautiful. Tall, long-limbed, cheekbones to die for, full cherubic lips that formed a perfect bow. And her eyes? A soft brown that reminded him of all the things that were bad for him. Rich espresso, expensive chocolate and hard, dark toffee.

Give her glasses trendier frames, or ultra-modern no frames—hell, even a set of contacts—and give her some clothes that flattered her figure and she'd be a damn knockout. So why? Why was a woman who would look good in a paper bag hiding herself away behind an over-sized white coat and polo-necked shirts?

He wandered towards her, intrigued despite himself. Isobella hadn't shown the slightest interest in him, and that in itself was enough to pique his curiosity. Without any vanity Alex knew that women were drawn to him. They *always* showed interest.

'What are you working on?' Alex asked as he approached.

Isobella felt the jump of muscles in her neck as his husky question abraded her sensitised flesh. She'd been hyper-aware of him wandering around the lab. No matter where he'd been, he'd always seemed to be in her peripheral vision, and the muscles of her shoulders were bunched tightly from forcing herself not to look. Being hunched over a microscope for two hours was not good health practice—as Alex had taken pains to point out.

She schooled her features, her fingers tightening around the base of the microscope as she looked up and gave him a polite smile. 'The software for Reg's presentation decided to go haywire this morning. I'm cross-checking the specimens against the graphics to make sure they correlate.'

Alex nodded, searching for a softening in her steady brown gaze. 'Did you get the Darwin sample yet?' he asked.

'This morning,' she confirmed. 'It's already catalogued and entered into the database.'

The database was extensive, comprising not just skin-scrapings from individual victims but actual tentacular material, and digital photos of the different stages of the dermonecrotic lesions caused by the tentacles of the box jellyfish as they adhered to their victims' skin.

'Was it a *Fleckeri*?'

'Yes. Would you like to examine it?' she asked politely.

He gave her a slow, measured look, as if he was searching for something, and she nervously lowered her eyes from the intensity of his gaze. Her vision was now level with the open neck of his shirt, and she found her eyes inexplicably drawn again to the fascinating scars.

'If it's not too much trouble,' Alex said, amused at her stilted formality.

'Of course. No trouble at all.'

Isobella rose stiffly from her high stool, not lifting her gaze, waiting for him to stand aside so she could pass by him to the fridges where the specimens were stored.

He took a step back, and she dragged in a calming breath as she retrieved the skin-scraping from earlier. She could feel his gaze on her back, and her fingers trembled as they closed over the specimen container.

She passed it to him wordlessly, taking great care not to make contact with him as she did so. He smiled his thanks and she returned it with a tight smile of her own relieved when he turned his back on her and set about preparing the slide.

What the hell was the matter with her? Two hours in the company of Alex Zaphirides and she was in a total dither. She didn't do dithering. Certainly no one she'd met in the laboratory world had been dither material. Mostly they were science geeks or maths nerds.

And that was what she liked about it. It was safe. Secluded. Nobody recognised her in here. Nobody asked inane questions or fluttered by half-naked, despairing that they'd run out of lipgloss. Nobody cared what label she was wearing, or whether her shoes matched, or what the light reading was. She was part of something much bigger. Worthwhile.

She watched him as he parked his very nice pin-striped butt on her high stool, and found herself wondering if he wore boxers or jocks.

Oh, for crying out loud!

'You'll need to adjust the magnification,' she said, for something to say to get her mind out of his trousers. 'I have it specially adjusted for my glasses.'

Alex twisted on the stool and looked at her. 'Thanks. I got it,' he said.

Idiot! Of course he would know that. Now he was probably wondering why on earth he'd hired a babbling dunce. She'd worked hard to prove that beauty could also come with brains. Worked hard to suppress the beauty part altogether. For God's sake, she hadn't worn make-up in sixteen years! She didn't want to blow all her hard-earned years of study and work because her seriously hot boss had resuscitated her long-dead libido.

'So, tell me about the case,' Alex murmured,

as he adjusted the magnification and the sample came into focus.

Alex's softly burred voice barely reached her from where she stood, and she moved reluctantly closer. She took a steadying breath and reeled off the facts as concisely and scientifically as she could.

'Eight-year-old female. Minimal exposure to the tentacles. Didn't require the antivenin or even hospitalisation.'

'Have we got parental consent to enter the little girl into the dermonecrosis study?'

Isobella nodded. 'Trish, our Northern Territory field officer, has arranged it. She'll follow up and chronicle the progression of the scarring for us. She's already e-mailed the first lot of photographs.'

'I'll take a look at them too, if you don't mind?' Alex murmured.

'Sure,' Isobella agreed faintly as she watched him work.

She went into more detail, grateful to be concentrating on the facts of the case and ignoring the waft of pure male aroma that emanated from Alex's body in tantalising waves. Every little movement in the chair, every twist of a dial, drifted more in her direction. He smelled of cut grass and wet earth and wild honey, and she had the strangest urge to bury her face in his neck just to see if his skin tasted as sweet.

His rumbling voice, occasionally interrupting to clarify a point or ask a question, was like hundreds of invisible fingers undulating seductively against her skin. Like the caress of an anemone swaying in tropical waters. She wanted to stretch. Close her eyes. Sigh. Purr.

'What was the weather like at the time of the envenomation?'

Alex waited a moment, and then looked up from the specimen when Isobella didn't reply to his question. Her eyes were shut, the heavy fringe of her lashes behind the glass just as fascinating as the rest of her. They fluttered and then opened, her brown gaze showing its first real emotion as it widened in shock. She opened her mouth to say something and a delicate shade of pink fanned her exquisite cheekbones.

'Why aren't you coming to dinner tonight with everyone else?'

Isobella shut her mouth and blinked at the rapid change in topic, her embarrassment at being caught with her guard down completely forgotten. Nematocysts, *Chironex Fleckeri*, statistical data—these were all things she could have answered questions on, had prepared to be questioned on. She hadn't been prepared for him to pry into her personal life.

She raised her hand to her throat, reflexively stroking the material covering her neck, strengthened by its presence. 'I...I don't...socialise...outside of work hours.'

It was true. Anyone present would have confirmed it for Alex. She just wished it didn't sound so...lame.

He quirked an eyebrow. She didn't socialise inside of work hours either. 'You are unhappy here? You don't like your colleagues?'

His gaze bored into hers. How was it possible to have eyes that blue? She lowered her gaze. 'I'm very happy here. I like them fine,' she dismissed.

Alex eyed her thoughtfully. Her discomfort was palpable. 'You have other plans? A date, maybe?'

Isobella frowned. 'Certainly not,' she said primly. Who did he think she was? Did he think she'd blow off a work function for a *man*?

Alex chuckled. She was so affronted he had no doubt she was telling the truth. 'Well, in that case I'm going to have to insist.'

Alex's husky laughter, even over a phoneline

from a thousand kilometers away, had always managed to turn her insides to mush. But this close she felt sure she was going to melt into a puddle right at his feet. There was no way she could sit at a table and have dinner with him. In fact she planned to avoid him for the rest of the week.

'Dr Zaphirides—'

'Ms Nolan?'

Isobella saw the slight lifting at the corner of his mouth and a dimple almost took her breath away. Damn him—she would not let him charm her.

'Alex. I've worked for you for two years. I'm here early every morning and I don't clock off till way past my time. Are you displeased with my work?'

'No.'

She almost sagged. His earlier criticism had left her with a nagging sense of insecurity. 'Then I believe the time after I leave the lab is my own. To do with as I wish.'

Alex bowed. 'But of course. Tonight, however, I'd like you to have dinner with me.'

Isobella knew he didn't mean him personally. But his cerulean eyes had a way of making her think she was the only person in the room. And he was so close, his wild honey and cut grass aroma wrapping her in a seductive web.

She opened her mouth to protest again, but he cut her off. 'Isobella.'

She felt goosebumps feather her skin as he elongated the vowel at the end of her name as he had done so often on the phone, his husky voice and slight accent a deadly combination.

'We are a team. It's a rare event to have us all together. We have made great progress towards our goals. I think a little team-building and a pat on the back for everyone is warranted once in a while. It's my thank-you to you all for keeping my Brisbane lab running smoothly. It would spoil everyone's evening not to have you there. You would do me a great service if you agreed to join us.'

Isobella doubted very much whether she would be missed. Oh, she knew she was respected for her work, but she doubted that anyone felt close enough to her to miss her socially. She had, after all, deliberately cultivated distance.

'Please, Isobella.'

His rumbled request weakened her resistance. Surely she could manage a few hours out of her comfort zone in the real world? One night out couldn't hurt, could it? She never went out. And the big boss had made a direct request. How churlish would it look to refuse his hospitality?

She became aware of how close they were standing. She took a step back and sucked in a deep breath. 'Certainly, Alex,' she acquiesced, with as much formality as she could muster. 'If you insist. Now, if you'll excuse me, I need to retrieve some documents from the printer.'

Alex inclined his head and watched her walk away, her back straight, her stride wooden, her reluctant acceptance rankling.

He should be pleased. So why did her I'd-rather-poke-myself-in-the-eye-with-a-sharp-stick demeanour bother him so much?

CHAPTER TWO

ISOBELLA got into the shower with an impending sense of doom. Damn Alexander Zaphirides and his *'Please Isobellaaaaa'*. Even now it washed over her as easily as the water sluicing over her skin, tightening her nipples, causing a heat down low that not even the cool shower could extinguish.

No, no, no. That was not why she had agreed to go out tonight. It had nothing to do with his husky request. Or the way he looked. Or his wild honey smell. It was strictly a business affair. Accepting his gesture of thanks as everyone else was. And he *had* insisted.

Thank God he was only here for the week, if this was how much havoc he'd created in just one day. On Friday he and Reg were going to the symposium in Cairns, and then he would be flying back to Melbourne.

She only had to get through the next few days.

Or she could take some sick leave—God knew she had a mountain of it. Plead a mysterious illness. The presentation was essentially complete, so her absence wouldn't cause too much disruption.

She switched off the tap hard and dried herself briskly. Who was she kidding? Her? Off work for a few days? She *never* took time off. She hadn't had a single sick day in her time with Zaphirides Medical Enterprises. Not even last winter, when she'd caught a really bad flu and had felt like death warmed up. Hell, she hadn't pulled a sickie—ever. Taking a few days off would cause an immense stir.

She was just going to have to get through the week as best she could. Her infatuation with him was ridiculous. There was absolutely no point getting herself into a dither over a man that she was never going to have. She'd resigned herself to her asexual existence many years ago, and no one had ever tempted her out of her self-imposed celibacy. She wasn't about to let a man who looked as if he could have his pick of beauties ruin her hard-won reputation.

Isobella wrapped the towel around her, anchoring it under her arms, and wandered into her room. She felt edgy and stared at the clothes in her wardrobe, wondering what the hell she was going to wear. Damn it, she *never* thought about what she had to wear any more. She had a cupboard full of high-necked garments, and she usually just put her hand in and picked one.

But then she hadn't gone out socially in years with anyone outside her family. And she never had to give too much thought to what she wore to work. Loose and comfortable were essential, and it was always covered by her white coat anyway. Fashion just didn't come into it.

The fact that she always dressed to hide and camouflage her figure and that tonight she was thinking purely of fashion made her restless and annoyed. She was suddenly thinking of all the beautiful outfits she'd worn in the past. In another life. Coveting them and that time as she hadn't in years. Why? So she could attract Alexander Zaphirides?

A man whose abrupt, dispassionate dismissal of her this afternoon had left her in no doubt of his utter disinterest? His gaze had swept over her body as if she was of no more interest to him than a bug squashed on the pavement. It was crazy to entertain any other thoughts.

And she knew better than that. Paolo dumping her had been lesson number one. Anthony had been lesson number two. Even now the memory of Anthony's response, how he had recoiled from her, still had the power to crush her into the ground. She'd been foolish to dare even to think that a man could see beyond the physical.

She shut the cupboard in disgust, trying to beat back the memories, trying to not give the swell of despair that had overwhelmed her so often sixteen years ago any purchase. It was no use getting caught up in the bitterness and anguish of the past.

Except maybe as a reminder. Maybe a good hard look at herself would remind her that this infatuation with Alex was out of the question.

She stalked into her sister's room, heading straight for Carla's full-length mirror. Isobella only had a small high mirror in her *en suite* bathroom, preferring not to be reminded on a daily basis of her mutilated body.

She peeled the towel off her body, standing naked before the glass. She clenched her hands by her sides, still shocked by her appearance after all these years. How could she blame Anthony for his reaction when her first instinct was to run screaming away from herself too?

She forced herself to look, though. It was brutal—emotional shock therapy at its worst—but it was also just what she needed. She wasn't Izzy Tucker the high-flying international model any more. She'd made the decision at nineteen to turn her back on that world jaded by hypocrisy and the relentless pursuit of beauty. And she'd been at peace with her choice and excited about starting a new phase of her life.

But she hadn't been prepared for the final cruel blow that had taken her controversial decision to turn her back on a successful high-profile modelling career and punished her for it. Her life as she had known it had ended during a photo shoot on an idyllic North Queensland beach sixteen years ago. In fact it had nearly ended full-stop.

The evidence still taunted her today, as she gazed in the mirror. Her nudity didn't register. All she could see were the marks where a box jellyfish, a *Chironex Fleckeri*, had wrapped its tentacles around her waist, disfiguring her, branding her with its ugly signature. And almost killing her in the process.

The purple whip-like scars that criss-crossed her abdomen were as mean-looking as ever. They'd faded a little over the years, but essentially each tentacle had left its savage mark, causing a permanent welt and marring the once sought-after bikini body that had graced many a magazine cover.

Isobella trembled with the effort it took not to look away in disgust. It had been a cruel twist of fate to have her career end on such a note, instead of on the high she'd imagined. At nineteen, being selected as a *Sports Illustrated* swimsuit model had been a major coup, and the perfect ending to a stellar career. And then it had all gone to hell.

Isobella secured the towel around her, unable to look any longer. She collapsed back on her sister's bed, staring at the ceiling, allowing herself to wallow in self-pity for a moment or two. It had been a long time since she'd let herself be pulled back into the awful quagmire of grief. A tear squeezed out from behind her lids and she let it trek down across her temple.

Damn Alexander Zaphirides. She hated this. It was his presence that had unsettled her so much. Here she was feeling sorry for herself when in reality she'd been exceedingly lucky. For one, she'd survived, and from what she'd been told, things had been touch and go for quite a few weeks.

And for another, her decision to leave modelling had already been announced, and she'd been happy and excited about embarking on a new career. She'd already made the mental shift away, preparing herself for a new chapter in her life. Had she been counting on continuing modelling when she finally awoke from her drug-induced coma she would have been very disappointed. The phones had stopped ringing. A disfigured model was no good to anyone.

Over the years she'd managed to develop a philosophical outlook to the incident. An acceptance, even, that there had been a grand plan for her—a destiny, a fate bigger than hers, beyond her control.

That was why she believed so much in the research that Alex was conducting. Helping to find a topical treatment for the dermonecrotic lesions caused by *Chironex Fleckeri* before they scarred its victims permanently. To date there had been no agent identified to reduce the long-term scarring, and she was at the forefront of the research.

It had been almost a calling from a divine force when she'd seen the advertisement just over two years ago. She'd been working in burns scarring research, but had known instantly the dermonecrosis study was her destiny. It was too late for her—but for future victims? It had been a challenge, a calling she hadn't been able to deny.

And nothing had swayed her from that path for two years. Nothing. Not thoughts of her past or of the unfairness of life or the vile flu. She'd had her face glued to a microscope, obsessively stalked the world wide web, and stayed back way too many nights leaving no stone unturned.

But now, tonight, with the prospect of having to socialise with a man who was sexier than a hundred Greek gods, she wanted to be beautiful again. To be Izzy again. If even just for a night.

Damn it. Damn her vanity to hell!

'Hey, babe? Are we having a slumber party?'

Carla? Her plane wasn't due back until later tonight. Was it? Isobella dashed away the moisture beneath her lids. She gave a shaky laugh, not bothering to rise from the bed. 'Sure, if you like.'

She looked up as Carla came into her line of vision. She looked as professional as she always did in her stewardess uniform. Her sister frowned down at her as she pulled her shirt out of the waistband of her skirt.

'Move over,' she ordered, and flopped back onto the mattress like a felled tree next to her.

'Exhausted?' Isobella asked as she watched Carla shut her eyes and give a deep contented sigh.

'No.' Carla shook her head. 'What year is it?'

Isobella laughed, and could have hugged Carla for arriving home at the precise moment she needed a pick-me-up. 'Poor Carla. Flying around the world, staying in gorgeous hotels, waiting on rock stars and screen gods. Italy is so hard to take this time of year.'

Carla laughed too. 'I'm afraid I pulled the economy section this time. Crying babies and a group of soccer hooligans who tried to set a new record for the most beer consumed on a transatlantic flight.'

Isobella laughed again, and they both lay looking at the ceiling for a while.

'So?' Carla said. 'What's up?'

Isobella exhaled a pent up breath. 'Dr Alexander Zaphirides, that's what.'

'Good grief!' Carla's head turned and she looked at her sister. 'That's right. Sorry—I'd forgotten McHusky was in town.'

Isobella smiled. Carla was the only person she'd ever confided in about her infatuation with her boss's voice. And her sister had nicknamed him very aptly.

'Is he as gorgeous as his voice suggests?'

Isobella nodded miserably. 'I think he's the most beautiful man I've ever seen.' And she had seen some very beautiful men.

Carla raised herself up on an elbow and looked down at her sister. 'Hah! Told you,' she crowed.

'I'm having dinner with him tonight.'

Carla sat up and stared at her sister incredulously. 'You are?'

Isobella shrugged her slim shoulders. 'He insisted.'

'Well, I like him already.'

'Don't get too carried away. The whole team will be there.'

'But still,' Carla grinned. 'You and McHusky.'

'Carla, be sensible,' she chided, absently rubbing her finger over the small scar in the centre of her neck. 'Nothing good can come of this.'

'Well, I don't know about that. He's finally getting you out of this house. Pulling you out of your comfort zone. For that I think the man deserves a medal.' Carla jumped up. 'Come on, let's get you ready. What are you going to wear?'

'I haven't got anything to wear,' Isobella murmured, feeling so depressed she just wanted to crawl into her bed and pull the covers over her head. 'I think I'll just plead a headache and stay home.'

Carla regarded her sister seriously. 'Izzy. What harm can it do?' she asked softly.

Isobella looked at her sister, flinching slightly at the childhood endearment—the name that had been on every designer's lips back in her heyday.

Was Carla mad? What if she wanted more?

She'd trained herself to not want more. Of anything. She didn't want to open the lid on a whole bunch of cravings she'd kept tightly locked away.

Carla lay back down on the bed. 'Not all men are like Anthony, babe. You have a great figure. Stop hiding it.'

Isobella snorted. 'I *had*. Past tense.'

'Your figure is as divine now as it was when you were storming those Paris catwalks.'

Isobella heard the slight trace of envy in Carla's voice. The sisters were chalk and cheese in the looks department. Carla was shorter and curvier, and although her figure was trim she always struggled to keep weight off. Isobella could, and did, eat like a horse, with no negative side effects whatsoever.

'You know what I mean,' Isobella replied.

'Babe. Any man worth his salt won't care about what you look like with your clothes off,' Carla said gently.

Isobella shook her head incredulously at Carla, knowing full well that the male of the species usually judged women exactly on what they looked like under their clothes. 'I look hideous!'

Carla shook her head. 'God. Once a model always a model. You have such a screwed-up body image, babe. So, your body's not what it was? But you are far from hideous. Your scars are part of you. You can lock yourself away because of them or live despite them. Beauty is more than skin-deep, and any man who judges you for the marks on your body isn't worthy of oxygen.'

Isobella knew what her sister was saying was right. She'd heard Carla and her parents say it a thousand times. She *did* have a skewed sense of beauty. She knew that. The international fashion scene was as catty as it was cut throat. It was hard to overcome how much it had screwed with her head.

'I know, I know.' She sighed. 'I just wish...I wish it had never happened.' Another tear squeezed out from beneath her lids and she wiped it away. It had been years since she'd uttered those words. *Damn Alexander Zaphirides!*

'Me and you both, babe.' Carla raised herself up on her elbow. 'Not least of all because those first few weeks you spent in Intensive Care were so harrowing there wasn't a day that went by when we didn't think you were going to die. But here you are. Alive. Don't let it keep robbing you of your life.'

Yes, Carla was right. *She was right.* But even though she'd already decided to give up modeling, the whole reverse fairytale—the swan turning into the ugly duckling—had been a huge psychological blow. Her self-esteem had taken an even bigger hit than her body. Her physical scars had reduced slightly over time, but she still grappled with her mental ones every day.

'Now *up!*' Carla ordered, grabbing Isobella's arm. 'Let's find you something to wear.'

Isobella followed reluctantly, and stood passively while Carla hunted through her cupboard.

'Aha! This. You bought it and never wore it. It's perfect.'

Isobella looked at the dress Carla was brandishing. It was one of many things she'd bought over the years since the accident, despite knowing she'd never wear it. Mainly because she didn't socialize, but also because it revealed more than it concealed. But the female inside her had been unable to resist. The *Fleckeri*'s brand might have robbed her of her confidence, but it hadn't taken away her love for shopping or beautiful clothes.

It was the colour of a deep merlot, and was made from a fabric that clung in all the right places. Isobella shrank from it. 'No. It's too… It'll show my trachey scar… I can't possibly…'

'It's perfect,' Carla bossed.

The feminine side of her wanted to reach out and touch the very sexy dress, but Isobella knew if she touched it she'd be a goner. 'It's all wrong.'

'Why did you buy it, then?' Carla demanded.

Because it was beautiful. 'It's not the image I'm trying to project,' she said primly.

'McHusky is here for a few days, and then you won't see him again. Don't you want to at least make him drool a little?' Carla held up her thumb and index finger with a whisker of space separating them. 'It's one night, babe. Just one. Don't you want to feel like a woman instead of a nerdy, four-eyed lab geek?'

'Hey,' Isobella protested at her sister's blunt assessment. But she could hardly refute it. A 'four-eyed lab geek' was the image she'd meticulously presented to the world. 'I do not want to attract Alex.'

Carla shrugged. 'So do it for yourself. You just said you wished it had never happened. Put on the dress and pretend for one night that it didn't. Be Izzy again.'

Carla held out the dress, and Isobella felt herself reach for it against all her better judgments.

Alex wasn't sure what he'd been expecting from Isobella tonight. In fact he wouldn't have been surprised had she not shown at all. But secretly he'd hoped that maybe they'd all get to see a little more of the person beneath the coat and the glasses.

Unfortunately not.

He spotted her the second she walked in. She was late, and he'd been eyeing the doorway while making polite conversation with Roland about the project. She paused at the 'Wait here to be seated' sign, searching for their table.

She was wearing horrible baggy trousers and a shapeless shirt that flared down from a mandarin collar in an A-line and left everything to the imagination.

She looked around, her eyes darting from table to table. She seemed nervous, one hand clutching at her bag the other pushing her god-awful glasses back up her nose. Her left foot tapped, and she flinched as a man at a table near the door let out a booming laugh.

She was obviously uncomfortable as her gaze continued to flit around the room, and he started to wonder whether Isobella suffered from agoraphobia. She had seemed perfectly at home in the lab, albeit completely alarmed at his suggestion that she come out tonight. But here she looked completely out of place.

She finally spotted them, and he noticed her hesitation before she squared her shoulders and moved towards them. One thing was certain—Isobella Nolan did not want to be here.

Without the camouflage of the white coat he could see her legs were long and slender as she strode to the table but the second she stopped the layers of trouser material swallowed their shape.

Isobella was conscious of her colleagues all watching her as Alex stood and greeted her. His husky rumble rendered her powerless to move. Her nipples hardened as if he had reached out and trailed his fingers across her breasts.

'Sorry I'm late.' She addressed the table. 'I was…' *mentally hyperventilating* '…my sister held me up.'

'You're here now.' Alex nodded. 'We saved a seat for you.'

Isobella was pleased to see her legs were still obeying impulses from her brain, even if the rest of her body was not. The empty seat was directly opposite Alex, and she cursed Carla for delaying her departure.

She stroked her throat reflexively as she settled in her chair, reassured by the presence of the high collar. She nervously adjusted her glasses, pleased she had changed out of the dress after Carla had retired to her bed. The dress had looked amazing, and had felt so feminine against her skin, with its clingy fabric and plunging neckline. But she lacked the confidence to wear it. She would have felt exceedingly self-conscious in it, and she was already way out of her depth.

Luckily the same couldn't be said for her underwear. Lingerie was a major weakness of hers—always had been—and the feeling of soft satin and the rub of lace was one she freely indulged. Something had to compensate for the blandness of her lab wardrobe and the fact that no one at the table tonight knew the silken wisps that lay beneath her baggy clothes made the wearing of them bearable.

Conversation resumed at the table, and Isobella feigned interest. Reg was beside her, talking about the presentation, and she nodded and replied and made some suggestions on automatic pilot, while at the same time taking absolutely none of the discussion in.

She was aware of Alex's too frequent gaze on her. It felt heavy against her skin, and she wanted to look him straight in the eye and tell him to stop. What did he want from her? She was here, wasn't she?

His presence was just too disturbing by far. Every husky word and gravelly chuckle coming from his perfectly sculptured mouth vibrated the air currents around her, causing a feather-light friction all over her body that was as erotic as it was distracting. He was hitting a big ten on her McHusky scale, which only ramped up her nervousness several more notches.

It didn't help that he looked amazing tonight. He was wearing a shirt the exact shade of his cerulean blue eyes, which somehow managed to magnify his utter maleness tenfold. He hadn't shaved before coming out, and the light growth of stubble at his jaw drew her gaze like a helplessly addicted moth craved light.

When he laughed his face creased into irresistible dimples, and the skin around his eyes crinkled into little lines that she just wanted to reach out and touch. Smooth. Kiss.

And then there were the scars on his neck, fully displayed again. As Reg talked about Cairns she found herself thinking that if he only wore his shirt buttoned up, and a tie, they'd be completely covered. Why didn't he? She had the same urge to touch them as she did his eye crinkles. Feel their irregularity. Smooth them. Kiss them.

'I don't know, Roland,' Alex said to the man sitting beside him. 'I think it's a field that attracts a more mature workforce. Most people seem to come from other occupations into the lab. Take Isobella, for example. She was a nurse before becoming a research assistant.'

Tuned in as she was to the rumble of Alex's conversation, Isobella's head snapped up instantly.

'Really? I didn't know that,' Roland murmured.

She heard the surprise in Roland's voice and saw it mirrored all over his face. In fact the whole table was looking at her, as if Alex had just proclaimed she'd been a nun prior to joining the team.

Imagine their surprise had he announced she'd been on track to becoming the next supermodel.

Isobella looked at him. His blue eyes were challenging her to elaborate. Her cheeks grew warm beneath her colleagues' scrutiny, and her pulse pounded through her head. She thought at this moment she quite possibly hated Alexander Zaphirides.

Hated his supreme confidence and how comfortable he looked in this social situation, in contrast to the near panic that was sweeping through her own veins. She hated him for insisting she come tonight, dragging her out of her comfort zone and then putting her in the spotlight. She wanted to crawl under the table and hide from prying eyes.

How the hell did he know this stuff anyway? She'd gone through the interview process with his admin people, and whilst she assumed he'd had the final say she'd also assumed he'd taken their recommendation and approved her employment without more than a cursory glance at her application.

'Yes,' Isobella confirmed, uncomfortably aware of the growing silence. She wasn't used to being the centre of attention any more. She was used to fading into the background. She didn't want their interest piqued. 'For a while.'

'And what made you decide to jump ship?' Alex probed.

Conscious of everyone waiting for her response, Isobella squirmed. This was none of his business—none of their business. But avoiding the question would only serve to arouse further interest. After all, this was a social evening with colleagues. People talked about themselves in social situations.

Which was exactly why she avoided them.

Isobella suppressed a sigh. Where did she start without sounding like a complete loon? By saying that six weeks in hospital had given her a true appreciation for what nurses did? That it had been a natural progression for her, eager for a new career and jaded from the selfishness of modeling, to fall into that honourable profession? That she'd enjoyed being a nurse—in fact missed the patient contact more than she allowed herself to admit? But it had been too…social? And…open.

How crazy did that sound? Even if it was the truth. Her nursing colleagues, used to being entrusted with people's most personal details, had never really understood her desire to keep to herself. Their candidness and their expectation of it being returned had made her uncomfortable. Also, the uniforms had made hiding her tracheostomy scar really difficult. Civvies and a white coat had been an absolute dream.

'I enjoyed being a nurse very much,' she said primly. 'But…' Isobella adjusted her glasses. 'I wanted to try something different.'

Alex noted the nervous fiddle, and the way her gaze didn't quite reach his eyes. She was lying. He wanted to reach across the table, whip those god-awful glasses off her face and demand to hear the truth. He hated that she hid herself behind those dreadful, unfashionable, clunky frames.

'Did you have to retrain?' Roland asked.

Isobella nodded. 'I did a science degree, majoring in medical research.' Thanks to her modelling years she'd had a nice nest egg saved, and had been able to undertake her degree full-time and not have to worry about money.

'I was going to be an engineer at uni.' Reg joined in the conversation. 'Bored me stupid.'

Isobella could have kissed Reg for stepping into the conversation, sparking others to share their stories. Not that she heard what they were saying. She was conscious only of Alex's eyes on her. He knew. She could tell. Knew that she had fobbed him off. His Aegean gaze held hers and she was powerless to look away.

Alexander Zaphirides was a man who could see right past her reserve. And, frankly, it scared the hell out of her.

The meal and the conversation flowed around her for the next couple of hours, requiring very little input from her—thankfully. Most of the chat centred around the Cairns Envenomation Symposium, and Alex and Reg's scheduled visit to the Piccolo Island scientific station. The facility, situated on a small island north of Cairns, sent many box jellyfish specimens their way, and both men were keen to look around.

Isobella added very little, uncaring of the itinerary or any of the other topics. Her colleagues heeded her shuttered demeanour, but Alex felt no such compunction and drew her into the conversation with practised ease at every opportunity. Not even Isobella's guarded, progressively stilted replies seemed to daunt him. She knew he was doing it deliberately. And she knew he knew she knew.

Isobella finished her dessert and wondered what the time was, and if it was too early to leave. Just listening to his voice was its own brand of erotic torture, and she'd had more than she could take for one evening. Once or twice a week for a couple of minutes at a time was usually more than enough for her sanity. His voice, those eyes, made her want things she couldn't have.

'Have you got the time, Reg?' she asked quietly, turning to face him.

Reg turned his wrist. 'Nine-thirty.'

Isobella heard the slight puff in his reply and frowned. Reg was sweating and looking a little pale. Sure, it was November, but the restaurant was air-conditioned. 'You okay?' she asked.

Reg nodded. 'Heartburn's playing up,' he nodded, rubbing his chest.

Isobella nodded back. Reg wasn't the healthiest specimen of manhood she'd ever seen. He had a massive beer belly and lived on liquid antacid. He always seemed to be swigging on a bottle. She'd never pried into whether or not he'd ever had it checked out, because she didn't believe in prying. But he was looking particularly pasty just now. 'Have you got your antacid with you?' she asked.

'Nah. Left it at the lab. Probably time for me to mosey on home anyway. The wife doesn't like being in the house at night by herself. She's pretty annoyed about me going up north for the week. I think I'm in the bad books enough.'

Reg stood and made his goodbyes, and Isobella took the opportunity to depart also. 'Think I'll call it a night too,' she said, rising to her feet.

Alex rose, his gaze glittering his disapproval, telling her he knew she was chickening out. Isobella returned his look defiantly. He didn't own her, and she'd had enough of this charade.

'I'll see you tomorrow, Reg,' he said, turning his attention away from Isobella, holding out his hand. 'I'm really looking forward to attending the symposium with you.'

Reg nodded, and Alex frowned as he felt the sweatiness of Reg's palms. He looked at the man closely. 'You okay?' he asked.

Reg nodded briskly. 'Bloody heartburn.'

Isobella felt a prickle of unease as Reg turned and staggered a little.

'Reg?' Alex flicked a glance at Isobella, who was also regarding Reg with obvious concern.

Then Reg clutched his chest and let out a guttural moan, before sinking to his knees on the ground beside his chair.

'Reg!' Isobella sank down with him, a hand on his arm, knocking her chair over in the process.

Alex strode around the table and joined her as their work colleagues hovered around. 'Call an ambulance!' he barked, straining his voice as he positioned himself behind Reg, easing the man back to support him whilst reaching for Reg's pulse.

The fast, erratic pace was worrisome, and whilst Alex might not have practised real medicine in quite a few years, he'd never quite forgotten what a heart attack victim looked like. And Reg's pale, cold, clammy skin was a big red warning flag. The man certainly fitted the description of heart-attack-waiting-to-happen.

The entire restaurant stopped as Alex's hoarse demand sliced through their evening merriment, and then bedlam ensued as people gasped, some stood and at least one person from every table made an emergency call.

'Reg, have you ever had angina before?' Isobella demanded.

Reg groaned, still clutching his chest. 'No.'

'The pain? What's it like? Does it go anywhere?' she fired again.

'Down my…my arm,' Reg huffed. 'I feel like… like an elephant's sitting on my chest.'

Isobella glanced up at Alex. She looked away quickly, stunned that even in the midst of this crisis he could take her breath away. Reg cried out again, gripping his chest, and then slumped against Alex. Isobella shook him vigorously and called his name.

'It's no use. He's not responsive,' Alex said.

Her hand trembled as her fingers sought his carotid pulse.

'Anything?' Alex demanded.

Isobella kept her fingers in place, praying for a bound, a flutter, any movement against her fingers to prove that everything was okay. She shook her head and looked at Alex again. 'Nothing.'

They exchanged a look, both knowing this was a very bad development. If he'd lost his cardiac output so quickly then the heart attack must be significant.

'Clear some of these tables back.'

His voice might have been low but it was laced with urgent authority. He shifted so he could lie Reg on the ground. It was too cramped to do adequate CPR, and the paramedics were never going to get a trolley in here.

'I'll look after the airway,' Alex said to her. 'Can you do compressions?'

She nodded, her medical training coming back to her with surprising clarity. 'Pass me my bag,' Isobella said to one of her colleagues.

She fished in it and found the small sealed package she was looking for. 'Here.' She passed it to Alex.

Alex looked at the protector kit. 'Thanks,' he said, ripping it open to reveal a handkerchief-sized square transparent piece of plastic, with a central two-way mouthpiece to prevent the exchange of bodily fluids during expired air resuscitation. He inserted it into Reg's mouth and delivered his first two rescue breaths.

'What's the ETA on the ambulance?' Alex asked, pausing while Isobella performed the chest compressions.

'It'll be here in a few minutes,' Roland confirmed.

A waiter pushed through the crowd. 'Here,' he announced, 'we have this. Will this help? My boss had it installed last year, when our head chef had a heart attack.'

Isobella and Alex looked up to find the waiter holding a portable automatic defibrillator. At this particular moment it was worth more than the Holy Grail.

Alex grinned as Isobella kept up her chest compressions. 'Yes, sir, it most certainly will.' He relieved the waiter of the treasure.

Alex wasn't overly familiar with this type of unit, but he knew that once switched on it gave audible prompts and only delivered a shock if it deemed the patient's rhythm warranted it. It was designed for lay people to use, and at the moment it was Reg's best chance. Alex knew that early defibrillation was crucial to ensure the best outcome in this rapidly deteriorating situation.

He worked around Isobella, tearing Reg's shirt open and slapping the two adhesive pads in the indicated positions on Reg's cold, clammy chest. The automated voice on the machine asked them to cease CPR while it assessed the rhythm. They waited for the machine, and Alex tried not to notice the way Isobella's blonde fringe had fallen forward in his peripheral vision.

The machine prompted him to deliver a shock, and asked everyone to stand clear. 'Stand clear,' Alex said, raising his voice, cursing the gravelly wobble and the havoc the increased volume wreaked on his damaged vocal cords.

He put his arm out in front of Isobella's chest and urged her back further. The last thing he wanted to do was to electrocute her. 'Stand clear,' he repeated to the crowd as his finger hovered over the button.

When Alex was satisfied no one was in contact with Reg's body he hit the green button, and Reg's body arced as the electricity charged through him. The machine re-evaluated and prompted another shock, and Alex delivered the second one.

Finally Reg moved. He gasped and moaned and the entire restaurant seemed to breathe a sigh of relief. 'Welcome back, Reg,' Alex murmured as he helped Isobella roll the big man on his side.

He looked at her and she gave him a relieved smile. A totally candid, non-guarded, elated smile. It was exhilarating. He grinned back, pleased beyond measure to be finally seeing the real Isobella. It was only the wail of a siren breaking between them that stopped his sudden impulse to lean over and kiss her soft full lips in triumph.

The paramedics pushed through the crowd, and then it was a blur of activity as they applied oxygen and hooked the patient up to their own monitor. Reg was throwing worrying ectopics and having short runs of ventricular tachycardia as the paramedics hastily inserted an IV and administered some GTN spray under his tongue.

'Let's scoop him and go,' the female paramedic said. 'I don't like the look of his rhythm.'

Isobella and Alex assisted, and they had him on the stretcher and were loading him into the back of the ambulance in two minutes.

'Ring my wife,' Reg whispered to Isobella, pulling the oxygen mask aside.

'Yes, I will.' Isobella nodded, her anxiety increasing at the grey tinge to Reg's skin.

'I'm going with him,' Alex said to her.

'I'm so sorry about the symposium,' Reg groaned as they locked the stretcher into place.

'Don't worry about that,' Alex dismissed. 'Nothing is more important than getting you better.'

'You can ride in front,' the paramedic said to Alex as she slammed the back doors.

Alex nodded. He turned to Isobella. 'Well, that's one way to break up a party.'

Isobella gave him a weak smile as his voice scratched along her taut nerves. The adrenaline that had surged into her system during the crisis was making her even more sensitive to its sinful eroticism.

'Thanks for your help tonight.'

'It was nothing,' she dismissed.

He nodded. The ambulance engine roared to life. 'I need a favour,' he said, raising his voice to be heard over the noise.

Isobella hesitated, wary of the sudden gleam in his too intriguing eyes. 'Okay…?'

'I need you to come to Cairns with me.'

Isobella blinked. *What the—?* 'No.'

'It's not a request.' Alex grinned at her increasing look of horror. 'I'll have the tickets transferred,' he said, turning away.

Isobella gaped at him, watched him climb into

the cab. *No way.* No way was she going away for a week with him.

Absolutely not.

CHAPTER THREE

'GOOD morning, this is your captain speaking. Thank you for joining us today on Flight 103, bound for sunny Cairns. We're currently cruising at an altitude of…'

Isobella closed her eyes and let the announcement flow around her, still unable to believe she was sitting in a first-class seat, with Alex's arm occasionally brushing against hers.

'So you're just going to ignore me for the next two hours?'

The sound was low and husky near her ear, his warm breath fanning her cheek. Isobella gripped the arm of her chair and cursed her body for the blatant physical reaction his voice evoked.

She opened her eyes and looked at him, mustering a quiet resilience. 'Yes.'

Alex laughed as Isobella shut her eyes again. He examined her face. Her bone structure really was magnificent. Not even her horrible glasses could disguise the classic features. 'Anyone would think I'd asked you to Outer Siberia instead of on a first-class ride to one of Australia's premier tourist destinations.'

Isobella felt the slow flare of goosebumps individually prick at her skin and the languorous hardening of her nipples within the confines of her pink Chantilly lace bra. *Must* he speak?

'Most women would be ecstatic.'

She opened her eyes and pinned him with a hard stare. Did he think she was going to fawn all over him? Use this time away to get cosy with him? *She was here under duress and this was strictly business.* 'I'm not most women.'

That one he'd already figured out for himself. In the four days he'd been in her company she hadn't acted like any other woman he knew. She didn't flirt, lean in when she talked to him, pat him on the arm or even smile at him. She did her job with ruthless efficiency and avoided him like the plague.

He regarded her seriously 'Yes. I can see that.'

Isobella wasn't sure whether to be flattered or insulted, and she was annoyed that she even cared. She shut her eyes, removing his impossibly sexy face from her vision, and wished it was as easy to erase him from her thoughts.

'I'm really grateful that you've stepped into the breach like this.'

As if he had given her a choice. 'Yes, well, Reg's heart attack and triple angioplasty could hardly have been anticipated,' she said magnanimously. She had to remember that Alex was her boss. It was *his* project she was working on. Giving him a piece of her mind, though very appealing, wasn't wise.

'Still, I hope it didn't inconvenience you too much.'

She opened her eyes to find his cerulean gaze disconcertingly close. 'I'm here, aren't I?'

Alex nodded. 'I'd feel better had you not taken so much persuasion,' he said derisively.

Well, tough. He'd known she hadn't wanted to come. She wasn't in the business of making a grown man feel better about himself.

Her eyes shut again, and Alex suppressed a smile. Did nothing ruffle her? On one hand he admired her single-mindedness, but on the other…

He wanted to rile her—mess her up a bit. Find out what lay beneath her dreary wardrobe, the awful glasses and her prim, carefully chosen words. Find out why she'd lied at dinner the other night. Her *real* story.

'Would either of you care for a drink?'

Isobella opened her eyes and addressed the air hostess. 'No, thanks.' Not that the woman was remotely interested in her or her beverage requirements. The dazzling redhead only had eyes for Alex.

'And you, Dr Zaphirides?'

Isobella blinked. She knew his *name*? Had she taken the time to look it up on the passenger list? She watched as the redhead batted her eyelids at Alex. *Oh, please!*

Alex noticed Isobella's irritation, and injected all his energy into the smile he gave the hostess. 'Coffee, thank you.'

Isobella watched as his dimples deepened and his attraction quotient rose into the stratosphere. *Great!*

'Coming right up, sir.'

Isobella shook her head at Red's flirty gaze and exaggerated hip wiggle. She was going to have to put up with this for a week. Women fawning all over him. Spending the morning with him at the airport had been a big enough trial.

The check-in counter woman had looked at

him as if she could spread him on her toast, the teenage girl behind the coffee shop counter had stared at him as if he'd just stepped out of an Austen novel, and a grandmotherly cleaner had winked at him and given him an if-I-was-twenty-years-younger leer.

Although, to be fair, Alex hadn't seemed to notice any of it. He'd been polite and gentlemanly to all, including her. Maybe he was so used to being ogled that it didn't register any more? Or maybe he was truly unaware of his effect on women?

That was a new one for her. She'd spent her formative years surrounded by very good-looking men. All of them more than aware of their power. None of them, unfortunately, aware of their insufferable arrogance.

Although there was an arrogance about Alex too. But it was different. It wasn't based on his physical attributes or other frivolous, conceited notions. It seemed to come from deep inside. A confidence that seemed to define his every movement. Was it the knowledge that he was a world-class researcher doing vital work? Or was it just an innate sense of self?

The hostess leant over Isobella as if she didn't

exist, and placed Alex's coffee on his tray. 'Blow on it, sir, it's hot.'

Alex threw another smile the hostess's way. 'Just the way I like it.'

Red's laughter tinkled lightly around them, making Isobella want to reach for her sick bag. Did Carla flirt with her passengers like this? The stewardess moved on to the seats behind them, and Isobella was grateful for the reprieve from the heavy scent she must have bathed in before coming on duty.

The plane shuddered a little as it hit some turbulence, and Isobella grabbed for the arms of her seat, brushing Alex's arm in the process. She hated the stomach-dropping sensation of the split-second freefall and took some deep breaths.

'You okay?'

'Fine,' she said tersely.

'That's it!' Alex exclaimed, looking at her white-knuckled grip. 'You're a nervous flyer. That's why you didn't want to come.'

'No.' Isobella had been flying first class on her own from the age of fourteen. She'd racked up enough frequent flyer points to put even the most career-obsessed businessman to shame.

'Public speaking brings you out in hives?'

'No.' She'd pranced on catwalks with next to nothing on in front of total strangers and hundreds of cameras for a living. Opening her mouth fully clothed was a walk in the park.

'Boats, then?'

Isobella hesitated. 'No.'

'Ah-hah!' He honed in quickly on her slight pause. 'It is. Do you get seasick, or is it some sort of phobia?'

She plucked the in-flight magazine out of the pocket in front of her. 'It's not boats. I'm just not that…keen…on the ocean.'

Which was true. She wasn't looking forward to travelling to Piccolo Island. But of course there was the other terrifying thing about being away with Alex—like her completely stupid crush.

'Afraid of drowning? Sharks? A *Fleckeri* coming to get you?' Alex murmured.

Her fingers tightened on the page. She'd have to be the unluckiest woman in the world to fall victim to a *Fleckeri* twice. No, her fear wasn't rational. She knew that. But those few seconds when she'd been in the water, with the tentacles wrapped around her, those moments of intense paralysing agony, were burned into her psyche as indelibly as the brands on her torso.

Even now her heart pounded in her chest at the memory of those excruciating seconds when the nematocysts had adhered to her bare midriff, firing their hot, burning poison into her body. The pain alone had nearly killed her. It had certainly driven her screaming from the water in a completely automatic flight-or-fight response, collapsing on the sand seconds later at Paolo's feet.

She blinked hard to erase the image, and the lingering memory of the pain and encroaching darkness. 'I just prefer being on land.'

'We do have to take a boat to Piccolo. You know that, right? It is an island, after all.'

'Yes. Thank you. I was aware.' She had been trying to forget about it.

She had argued with Alex that it wouldn't be necessary for her to go on to Piccolo, that she could leave after presenting her paper at the symposium, but he had insisted. The Piccolo Scientific Station, situated on the northern fringe of the Great Barrier Reef, played an integral part in their research, and Alex had wanted Reg, and therefore now Isobella, to be familiar with its operations.

She flicked a page over with more effort than was required, the harsh snapping sound mirroring her irritation. Red passed by, and Isobella asked her for a set of headphones. Alex might have cornered her into coming to Cairns, but it didn't mean she had to like it or play footsie with him for a week.

Seconds later Red returned, with her eyes-only-for-Alex smile, dropping the headphones in Isobella's lap. Isobella plugged them in and pushed them into her ears gratefully, leaving the hostess to her flirting. She chose a hard rock station, roaring the sound up to a level way beyond safe.

Alex took the hint, smiling to himself as the hostess departed. *Good!* Finally Isobella seemed a little het-up. She'd shut her eyes again, and he was left to ponder why her het-up state should matter so much.

Why, contrary to all her don't-even-think-about-it signals, Isobella Nolan was becoming more intriguing by the minute.

Isobella woke to a gentle shake, and Mick Jagger screaming about not getting any satisfaction in her ear. Alex smiled at her as he indicated lunch was being served and she thought, *Get in line, Mick.* Suddenly, with his dark, dimpled good-looks filling her vision, all the lonely years seemed magnified. She removed the headphones.

'I'm sorry. I wasn't sure if you wanted to eat or not.'

'Oh, thank you. I'm starving.' Her stomach had been tied in so many knots this morning there'd been no way any food could have found room. Alexander Zaphirides was driving her to anorexia! Something even years modelling hadn't managed.

'I can't believe you can power-nap like that,' Alex murmured as he investigated the contents of the dish below the sealed foil. 'I need to be completely horizontal.'

Isobella shrugged as she picked up her knife and fork, trying not to picture Alex horizontal. In bed. Possibly naked. 'Old nursing skill.'

They ate in virtual silence, apart from the odd comment about the gourmet meal. Isobella devoured her food with gusto. It had been quite a few years since she'd eaten airline food, and she appreciated the fact that she no longer had to think about minding the calories or fat content. Not that she'd ever been especially good at that.

'Are you going to eat your roll?' Isobella asked

as Alex put his cutlery down, wiped his mouth on the linen napkin and placed it on top of the tray.

He shook his head. 'It's yours.'

'Thanks,' Isobella said, as she whisked it off his plate and slathered butter on it.

Alex raised an eyebrow. A woman who wasn't afraid to eat. Now, that was a change. He laughed.

Isobella looked at him, her mouth full of his bread roll. 'What?' she managed to get out around the contents of her mouth.

He shook his head. 'My mother would love you.'

Isobella swallowed. What the hell did she say to *that*?

Alex laughed again at her puzzled look. 'She's always telling my sisters and my nieces and nephews they don't eat enough.'

'You're an uncle?' Isobella asked, swallowing the last of the bread.

Alex frowned. 'Yes. Seven nieces and five nephews. Why? Don't I look like an uncle?'

Alex oozed single-man-about-town, in yet another expensive suit. Charcoal, with a deep purple shirt worn, as always, open at the neck *sans* tie. He looked rich and successful, and most definitely not uncle material. She couldn't imagine him kissing babies or changing nappies. 'Not really.'

'Well, I am. And a good one at that.'

She was surprised by the pride in his voice. He obviously enjoyed his role. If he was that fond of kids, why didn't he have a few of his own? Wasn't that what Greek men wanted? A boy to carry on the name?

Red stopped to collect their trays, and Isobella gave her a polite smile. Alex passed his tray up, reaching across her slightly, and Isobella felt her body hum in response to his. What would a child of Alex's look like? Dark hair and eyes and a chubby, cherubic face? Like a little dark angel?

'Do you want to go over our timetable for the week?' Alex asked, placing his briefcase on his now cleared table.

Isobella blinked. Anything. Anything to keep her mind off her sudden crazy desire to see Alex's son. 'Sure.'

'Okay. So, Saturday and Sunday is the symposium in Cairns. It kicks off tonight with welcome cocktails.'

Alex wondered if Isobella had brought anything suitable for a cocktail party. Did she even own anything that wasn't drab and two sizes too big?

'My paper on the effects *Fleckeri* antivenin has on dermonecrosis is on Saturday morning. Yours outlining the up-to-date study findings is on Sunday afternoon. Then on Monday we have the clinic all day. Did you bring the charts?'

Isobella nodded and opened her own brief-case. 'All twelve cases.'

Part of the research project involved following up as many past *Fleckeri* envenomations as possible. Recent stings were reasonably easy, but tracking down older cases had proved very difficult. People changed addresses, and quite a few box jellyfish victims had been overseas tourists.

But it was vital to the project to be able to get a good archive of pictures of the progression of the scarring over the years, and it was part of Isobella's job to track down the victims.

She'd found twelve who still lived in the Cairns area, and they were using this time up north to see those people, take a history, and gather more photographic data. To be able to build up a picture of the scarring as it evolved from the initial stages of dermonecrosis to the hallmark deep purple scars was invaluable to the study.

But it was another reason she wasn't looking

forward to this trip. Confronting other victims, hearing their stories and seeing their scars would be challenging.

Reg was supposed to be doing it.

'Did you manage to locate that model who was stung sixteen years ago? What was her name? Izzy someone?'

Isobella's hand stilled momentarily on her briefcase as her heart thumped loudly in her chest. 'Izzy Tucker.' She'd used her mother's maiden name when she'd been modelling.

This was too close for comfort.

'No. All my investigations led to a dead end.'

'Pity,' Alex mused. 'Her records are an impressive read—her abdominal scarring was quite extensive. It would be interesting to see all these years down the track.'

If only he knew... 'Do you want to go over these cases now?' Isobella asked, her fingers trembling on the front cover of the first chart.

'Nah, we'll have some spare time on the weekend.'

Isobella nodded, shaken by his reference to Izzy Tucker—to her—and grateful for the reprieve from what was difficult subject matter for her. Talking to those twelve people on the phone had been surprisingly trying. The longer she put off having to delve into their lives and reflect on her own misfortune, the better.

'On Tuesday we get a small plane to Temora Island, and then a boat to Piccolo.'

Goody, goody gumdrops. 'Excellent.'

Alex smiled to himself. She sounded as if he'd just announced they were parachuting into a desert for forty days and nights. With no rations. He placed the itinerary back in his briefcase and stowed it at his feet.

'Another coffee, Dr Zaphirides?'

Red was back, and Isobella found herself bristling at Alex's charm as he nodded his thanks. 'I'll have one too,' she called after the hostess.

The coffee was before them in record time. Alex reached across her slightly to take his from Red's eager fingers, and Isobella found her gaze drawn to the slashes on his neck—as they had been most of the morning. His open shirt and olive skin were in stark contrast to the thin white lines—it was hard not to notice.

She knew enough about scars to know that each one told its own story of torment and pain, and guessed that he must have suffered significantly. She wondered if it had been as bad as the scars seemed to suggest, and again found herself itching to touch them. Press her mouth to them.

'Why don't you just go ahead and ask?'

His husky query rumbled in her ear, and Isobella's startled gaze flew to his. *Damn!*

'I've noticed you staring at them quite a bit.'

She watched as he swept a hand down his neck, stroking the scars with the pads of his fingers. The rasp of his three-day growth against his palm was almost as enticing as the rasp in his voice.

She flushed. 'I'm sorry. I didn't mean to stare.'

Alex smiled and shrugged, used to people's interest. 'They're hard to miss.'

You could cover them up. Put on a tie. She checked her own scar was safely concealed by her polo-necked shirt before pulling her gaze from his and fixing it straight ahead on the seat in front. 'It's none of my business.'

'Aren't you at least curious?'

She was the least female woman he'd ever met. She didn't wear jewellery or make-up, she didn't gossip, and she definitely didn't flirt. Add to that a god-awful fashion sense and she was the full disaster. And yet her appeal grew by the second.

She shook her head. The man showed his scars

off to the world—that was way more evolved than she was going to get. She didn't feel up to a discussion on a subject she found too emotionally fraught at the best of times. 'It's really none of my business.'

Alex regarded her for a few moments. 'Come on,' he cajoled, dropping his head closer to her ear. 'There must be gossip at work about me.'

His voice rasped along her nerves. Well, *duh*! Of course there was. But how could he be so…so casual about it? So unaffected?

'Come on, Isobella. Tell me.'

'There are different versions,' she said awkwardly, dropping her gaze from the probing intensity of his blue eyes. But now she was looking at his throat again.

He chuckled. 'That does sound interesting. Tell me the more outrageous ones.'

Isobella shrugged, feeling ridiculous even repeating them. His scars were obviously surgical in origin. 'Knife fight and shark attack.'

Alex whistled. 'Wow, I *have* led an exciting life.'

He smiled at her, and she felt the magnetic pull of his deep dimples and Aegean gaze. Isobella was intrigued despite herself. Maybe it was the nurse in her. Or maybe it was the scarred young woman still grappling with the horrors of her own story.

'So what really happened?' she asked softly.

Alex's smile slipped. He absently stroked his neck, thinking back to the events that had changed the entire course of his life. All the things he'd taken for granted—his career, his voice, the woman he'd loved—had all been ripped away from him in a few short months.

The silence stretched between them, and Isobella worried that she'd overstepped a line. She better than anyone understood how difficult it was to tell some stories. His smile had disappeared and his blue eyes looked suddenly bleak.

'I'm sorry—forgive me. Really…it is none of my business.'

'I had throat cancer.'

There. He'd said it. He'd never told anyone the truth before. He knew it perpetuated the outrageous rumours, but he preferred them to having to relive the horror of it all. Quite why he was even telling her was a mystery.

Isobella shut her eyes briefly as her nursing background filled in all the gory details. She wanted to ask how—he was young and didn't smoke—but all she could do was gasp.

'Oh, Alex.' She clutched her throat.

Alex found her compassion captivating. He stilled as the hushed anguish in her voice washed over him. The white noise of the cabin faded until there was just her and him. Her brown gaze, usually carefully schooled, radiated shock and empathy. The aloofness he so often saw in her eyes fell away. The hardness liquefied until he was staring into a bottomless pool of rich, dark molasses.

It was as if she knew what he'd been through. As if she'd been right there with him. Why was it that he felt more empathy from Isobella in this moment then he'd ever felt from the woman who was supposed to have loved him?

'How long ago?' she murmured

Alex hesitated. He'd already shared too much with almost a total stranger. 'Ten years.'

Isobella felt the beginnings of a strange connection with him. She didn't want to, but it was there anyway. She too had looked death in the face and conquered it. She too still bore the marks of her battle with mortality.

There was so much she wanted to ask him. About the surgery and whether he'd needed chemo, if he'd been given the all-clear, but his face was shuttered, an untouchable mask. It was as if he already regretted telling her what he had.

She glanced at his neck again. His trachey scar, thick and ugly, dominated the finer L-shaped scar. The thought that he might never have made it was suddenly appalling. She couldn't help herself. She lifted her hand off the armrest and slowly reached out.

The roughness of his stubble grazed her fingers, and she shivered as they came to rest against his scar. Her other hand reflexively encircled her own throat as she pressed the puckered flesh gently, feeling it give a little.

'Does it hurt?' she asked quietly, mesmerised by the feel of it.

Alex didn't dare move, didn't dare even breathe as her finger brushed against his skin. It was such a fleeting caress, but he couldn't remember being more affected by a woman's touch. 'No.'

His voice sounded huskier than ever, and she felt the rumble of it vibrate through her fingertips. His neck was warm, and she could see the bound of his pulse at the base of his neck. She stroked the pad of her thumb against it.

'Good afternoon, ladies and gentleman, this is

your captain speaking. We'll soon be beginning our descent into Cairns. If you could follow the instructions of the cabin crew we'll have you safely on the ground in about twenty minutes.'

Isobella blinked. She withdrew her hand, his skin suddenly scorching, and sat back, acutely aware of how close their heads were.

'I'm…I'm sorry,' she said, mortified, her face flaming. She stared at her hand in her lap, trying to fathom how it had ended up on Alex's neck.

'Don't be.'

She glanced up at him. His blue gaze was gentle. And then Red came along and asked them to place their seats upright, and Isobella was glad to see her for the first time. Even her attempt at flirting didn't irk—especially when Alex politely declined her invitation to drinks later that night.

It shouldn't matter to her who he flirted with. But suddenly it did.

It was the worst kind of insanity.

CHAPTER FOUR

THE top-floor suite Isobella had been allocated was breathtakingly sumptuous. A king-sized four-poster bed, Balinese-style, with a filmy white canopy that floated down the sides dominated the room. Layers of fat pillows, dark cane lounge chairs and earthy seagrass rugs added to the decadence.

A rattan ceiling fan circulated lazily, billowing the bed's curtains. Dark wooded occasional tables were scattered throughout, displaying stone Buddhas. Vases of frangipani and rattan lamps added unique touches.

It had been years since she'd stayed in such luxury, and, looking around the room, she realised that a small part of her missed the trappings of her former life. The thought irritated her. She had done better work in the last few years than in all the years she had posed for cameras.

The conference centre was on the Cairns ocean front, and the one-hundred-and-eighty-degree view from her balcony was magnificent. She stepped out, admiring the tranquil swell of the ocean, the waves undulating rhythmically against the shore. The cloudless sky was fairy-floss blue, and it was hard to believe that a low pressure system was hovering a few hundred kilometres out to sea.

Isobella inhaled a breath of salty air, turning her face towards the sun. She thrived on her cloistered life in the lab but, like any good indoor plant, occasional exposure to the sunshine was vital for life. She just wished it hadn't been Alex who had uprooted her and was now firmly planted in the next-door suite.

She wandered back inside and unzipped her bag, planning to unpack and then fire up the Internet and continue her literature search. On the top, carefully folded with a note pinned to it, was the dress that Carla had wanted her to wear to dinner the other night.

Isobella grimaced, detaching the note. Carla was nothing if not persistent.

This has cocktail party written all over it. Dance with McHusky for me. I dare you.

She touched it. The material felt cool and soft against her fingers. Tempting. Seductive. She felt like Alice, confronted with the 'eat me' note. Or Eve, staring down the serpent. Damn Carla and her meddling.

Isobella ignored the dress, pushing it aside as she pulled all the other garments out and deftly hung them in the wardrobe. It only took a few minutes, and she zipped the bag up again, still containing the dress and her scraps of under-wear, stowing it on the luggage rack. Even if temptation got the better of her the dress would be too crinkled to wear. And Isobella made it a policy *never* to iron.

A sea breeze blew through the open balcony doors as Isobella sat at the desk and booted up her laptop. She could log on to work via her remote access password and continue where she'd left off. She felt resentment at being removed from the lab bubble in her blood. Every day away from her microscope was one day further from their goal.

The phone rang, and she picked it up as she navigated her way through several passwords. 'Hello?'

'I'll pick you up at six sharp.'

Isobella blinked. Alex's gravelly voice lent a sinfulness to the perfectly innocent statement. So much so that she almost acquiesced. She shut her mouth, catching herself before she agreed. 'I don't think I'll go,' she said, clearing her throat, injecting a steadiness she didn't feel with his husky request still tingling in her ear.

'Isobella—'

'It's not necessary.' Her eyes were drawn to the brilliant sparkle of the mid-afternoon sun on the ocean.

'Isobella—'

'You don't need me there. I'd rather work on the analysis of data from the latest batch of samples.'

Alex was man enough to admit that it wasn't a question of need. He wanted her there. Period. 'You are part of this symposium. You are presenting a paper, and you are also representing Zaphirides Medical Enterprises and our research. People will expect you. And while you're on my dollar I expect you to attend all functions.'

'I didn't want to be here, Alex.'

'But you are.'

'You know damn well if Reg hadn't had a heart attack I wouldn't have been.'

'Why do you do that? Why let Reg take the credit for your work?'

'It's *our* work. We're a team, remember.' It honestly didn't matter to her—as long as they were able to find a treatment for the *Fleckeri* scarring.

'You put the presentation together, didn't you?'

'Yes.'

'And while everyone else is busy with their projects you practically run the dermonecrosis research single-handed.'

'Reg works on it too. And some of the other researchers help from time to time.'

'But it's basically your project.'

Isobella felt a little thrill at his acknowledgement. It made her proud to be granted ownership, no matter how fleetingly. 'He's my boss, Alex. One of the perks, I guess.'

Alex bristled. 'No. *I'm* your boss. And I'll be at your door at six.'

Isobella heard the dial tone in her ear and looked at the receiver, cursing herself for her gaffe. But—damn it all—he knew what she meant. She replaced the phone, drawing on the steady beat of the waves against the shore for strength.

Another awful creation assaulted him as Isobella's door opened.

'How long does this thing go on for?' she asked.

He almost laughed. She was so comical, standing there with her annoyed expression knitting her delicate brows together, in her standard drab shapeless trousers and blouse complete with god-awful bow at the neck.

And it wasn't a bow that was meant to entice. To make a man wonder whether, if he tugged it, it would unravel to reveal wispy lace and bare skin. No. It was a bow that would have looked quite at home on a big, fat Christmas wreath. She reminded him of an eighteenth-century spinster, and he grappled to understand why he found her so intriguing.

'Good evening to you too, Isobella.'

His voice stroked along tense muscles, tightening them further. She rolled her eyes as she pulled her door shut. 'Good evening, Alex. How long does this thing go on for?'

'A couple of hours.'

They made their way to the lift, with Isobella plotting how she could leave early and Alex wondering if her entire symposium wardrobe was as bad. The lift arrived and they entered the car.

The doors slid shut and he looked at her downcast head. 'There's going to be a lot of industry people here tonight. A lot of money looking for worthwhile projects to back. Please try and look like your enjoying yourself,' he said derisively.

Isobella glared at him. 'Don't worry. I know the drill.' She might never have been to one of these parties, but Reg had talked about the schmoozing *ad nauseam*.

'Good,' he said, tight-lipped. The lift doors opened and he held out his arm for her in an automatic gentlemanly gesture. For a moment he thought she was going to snub him and he suppressed a smile when she reluctantly took his arm.

She dropped it as soon as they entered the cool elegance of the Daintree Room, where a couple of hundred people all dressed in their finery milled around, drinks in hand. The delicate strains of a string quartet floated around the room, and a waiter presented them with a tray of drinks as soon as they settled in one spot.

Isobella grabbed some champagne, feeling a little claustrophobic from the huddle of bodies around her and the noise of two hundred people all conversing at once. The urge to down it in search of some Dutch courage was strong, but, as panicked as she felt, Isobella wanted to keep a firm grip on her sensibilities.

Alex was looking a particularly devastating form of wonderful, and she didn't dare give her infatuation any rein tonight. He was certainly the best-looking man in the room. His presence was commanding, and even amongst the noise of the crowd she was tuned in to the low gravelly timbre of his voice as if they were the only two people in the room.

People drifted towards them, and a small circle of delegates surrounded them, seemingly for the duration. Alex seemed to know everyone, and he was the epitome of charm as he introduced her around. After her initial misgivings, Isobella relaxed and enjoyed herself. She was, after all, talking on a topic very close to her heart. She could talk about her project all night.

'Ah, Jenny!'

Isobella looked up from her conversation with a general practitioner to see Alex kissing the cheeks of a gamine strawberry blonde. She gave him a warm hug, and laughed at something Isobella couldn't catch.

'Isobella, come and meet Jenny,' Alex interrupted.

'Hi.' Jenny smiled, holding out a hand. 'I'm Jenny Bosworth.'

'Oh, hi,' Isobella said, returning the friendly smile and trying to not act starstruck. Jennifer Bosworth was an eminent expert in the field of marine envenomation. 'It's a pleasure to meet you, Dr Bosworth. I'm really looking forward to your paper on Portuguese Man O' War behaviours in Hawaiian waters. Your data on envenomation and anaphylaxis was amazing.'

'Thank you,' Jenny said. 'I can't wait to hear where you're up to in your study.'

Isobella blushed. Jennifer Bosworth was interested in *her* research?

'Jenny and I go way back,' Alex explained, grinning down into his colleague's face. 'In fact it was a trip to Hawaii that got me interested in this field of research.'

Isobella nodded, noticing that Alex's arm was around Jenny's back, his hand resting on her hip.

It looked very intimate. Were they more than colleagues?

'Alex was on a Hawaiian beach when a Man O' War claimed another victim. A six-year-old male. He came to see the little boy the next day and we got talking.'

'We've consulted a lot over the last couple of years.'

Isobella smiled while they chatted, watching their easy interaction. She'd never seen Alex this candid. They were obviously friends. *Close friends.*

Jenny was called away, and was quickly replaced by the CEO of a company that had donated a substantial amount of money to Alex's projects after his teenage grandson had been stung by a *Fleckeri* a few years back. Alex updated him on the project, and invited the company director to a guided tour of the Brisbane facility.

Isobella was content to sit back and watch. And listen. Hell, the man could read the *Concise Oxford Dictionary* to her and she'd listen. His professionalism was outstanding. He could quote figures and summarise reports and give educated opinions on all aspects of his operations. He knew what every one of his staff were doing, and their up-to-date findings. He had an air of authority that no one questioned.

'Alex Zaphirides! Oh, my God, it *is* you!'

Isobella saw Alex's jaw clench slightly, and turned to look in the direction of the voice as the CEO excused himself. A curvy siren with glossy long black hair, plush cherry lips and a killer cleavage sashayed towards him.

Alex stared. *This could not be happening.* 'Sonya?'

He did that polite old-fashioned inclination of his head thing again, but not before Isobella noticed his Aegean gaze frost over. In fact everything about him had become rigid, even his usually deadly smile. It barely made an impression on his dimples.

The woman stepped right into Alex's personal space, tottering on her sexy six-inch heels. She lifted herself on her tippy-toes, slid her hands up his jacket front and pressed her pouty mouth to both of Alex's cheeks. 'I do declare,' she said, wiping away her lipstick brands, 'you're looking fab. It's been too long, Alex.'

Not long enough as far as he was concerned. He removed her hand and was pleased to see her smile slip a little.

'Time flies, Sonya.' *When you're having surgery and radium and worrying about whether you'll see next year and your life is generally falling apart.* 'May I introduce one of my colleagues, Isobella Nolan?'

Isobella took an instant dislike. This woman redefined fawning. Her scarlet fingertips clung to Alex's lapel and she had the uncharacteristic urge to bat them off. Jenny's familiarity had been intriguing, but this woman's was plain suffocating.

Sonya gave Isobella a brief dismissive once-over. 'Sonya Nikolaidis. Do you mind if I butt in? I knew Alex back when he was surgeon.'

Isobella took the proffered hand and shook it distractedly as she madly tried to process the information about Alex being a surgeon. The other woman was patently uninterested in Isobella's preoccupied state, quickly turning her full attention back to Alex, and Isobella figured it wouldn't have mattered a jot if she had objected to the interruption. Something told her Sonya Nikolaidis always got her man.

Even though Alex was grim-mouthed, his face a picture of foreboding, they looked stunning together. Their Greek backgrounds were more obvious together than separately. Just how well had Sonya Nikolaidis known Alex? Intimately, by the look of her body language. Her body seemed perfectly at ease in Alex's personal space, leaning into him, and her gestures were indicative of a carnal familiarity.

Alex kept himself rigid, wanting nothing more than to tell her to get the hell away from him, but he had no doubt that Sonya could still cause a scene. And he had absolutely no intention of betraying how very much her desertion still rankled.

'What are you doing here, Sonya?' He injected a deliberate note of boredom into his enquiry. Unfortunately for him, Sonya's ego had always been able to withstand the impact of a truck.

'I've been a pharmaceutical rep for years. I'm in management now. I work for MediCorp.'

But of course. Alex clenched his fists. Only the largest supporter of Australian-based research and drug development in the land. When they did find the magic formula to help box jellyfish victims with their scarring he'd need MediCorp's backing to produce it. 'Congratulations.'

'I hear you're big in the jellyfish biz?'

Alex gave her a brisk nod. Nothing like reducing valuable scientific research to a three-word catchphrase. What had he ever seen in her? Even now her ambition was palpable.

'Dance with me, Alex.'

Alex looked down into Sonya's expertly made-up face. Her lips were glistening a deep red, her eyes ringed with dark kohl and fringed with heavily enhanced lashes. Her gall was amazing. Did she seriously think that time had reduced the wounds she'd inflicted? That he'd jump at her request? 'Actually, I'd just asked Isobella. If you'll excuse us?'

Isobella, who had been watching their exchange in uncomfortable silence, almost choked on her sip of champagne. Alex took the glass from her suddenly nerveless fingers, placed it on a passing waiter's tray and took her hand, tugging her towards the dance floor.

'Alex,' she whispered, scurrying to keep up with his determined stride so she wouldn't fall flat on her face, 'what the hell are you doing? I didn't come here to dance.'

He continued leading her doggedly towards the area where the string quartet were playing and some people were already dancing.

'I'm not dancing with you,' she protested again in a vicious whisper as they reached their destination.

Alex smiled down at her. 'Oh, yes, you are,' he said, swinging her around and pulling her towards him.

Isobella automatically grabbed for his shoulder to steady herself, and before she knew it he had his arm around her waist and their hands were linked. 'Smoke Gets in Your Eyes' started up, and he pulled her closer.

Unlike Sonya, Isobella was not comfortable in Alex's personal space, and she held herself rigidly as far away from him as she could in the circle of his arms.

'Relax, I'm not going to bite,' he said irritably.

Even grumpy, his voice caused an eruption of goosebumps, as if he had indeed nuzzled her neck and taken a bite. Isobella glanced at his bleak mask to snap her out of the dangerous fantasy. *Bad move.* His dark mood just enhanced his attractiveness.

She looked down, her gaze at his throat, his scars tempting her too in their own bizarre way. Ever since she'd touched them earlier on the plane they'd grown in fascination tenfold. She wished this was a real dance. A dance between lovers. She could have nestled her head on his shoulder and nuzzled his neck, caressing the scars with her lips.

She looked away impatiently, focusing squarely on his shoulder and the dark fabric of his suit. She was excruciatingly aware of the intimacy of the music, of their closeness, of the heat coming off his body and the wild honey smell of his aftershave seducing her at every turn around the floor. She sucked in a steadying breath and was dismayed by its raggedness.

She had to say something. This silence while their bodies swayed inappropriately, just shy of touching, was crazy. 'So who's Sonya?'

Alex's hand tightened on her hip. 'My ex.'

Isobella looked up at him, shocked by the admission and the bitterness in his gravelled tone. His brow had furrowed, his smile had become taut, his sexy dimples were flattened into solemn lines. *Yep—just the cold bucket of water she needed.* 'You were married?' she squeaked. No wonder they'd looked so good together.

He looked down into her unadorned face through the awful owlish glasses and thought how much he preferred Isobella's classic understated beauty to Sonya's high-maintenance glamour. 'Ex-fiancée,' he corrected grimly.

His top lip furled. It hardened his features, and she got a glimpse at the arrogant surgeon he'd probably been back in his heyday. She dragged her gaze from his, focusing on his shoulder again. So Sonya and Alex had been engaged.

'What happened?'

He didn't look at her. His grip on her hip had started to bite, and the rigidity of his frame now matched hers. His face was shuttered and the silence stretched between them.

'Alex?' Why she felt compelled to push, she wasn't sure.

'Let's just say she preferred me when I was a surgeon.' *Not so much when I was undergoing radium, throwing up, losing my hair and being generally angry at the world.*

He still hadn't looked at her, but he radiated hostility, the huskiness of his voice adding an extra degree of indignation. Isobella started to get the feeling that Sonya had deserted him when he'd most needed her. She thought about Paolo's desertion, and how much it had torn at her heart, at the fabric of her life and all she'd thought she'd known about herself and their love.

'I'm sorry.'

The emotion in her whisper was compelling, and he glanced at her sharply. She had that soft empathy in her gaze again, that molasses quality. Eyes a man could drown in. For a moment he felt enveloped by her compassion.

He shrugged, trying to lighten the mood. Her empathy was seductive. 'It was a valuable lesson.'

It sounded so hard, the words delivered with a gravelly bleakness she couldn't help but shiver. 'Plenty more fish in the sea?' she said, injecting a lightness into her tone. This was too deep, too personal, for both of them.

'Oh, no. I may be Greek, but I'm not worth a damn as a fisherman. These days all I do is catch, kiss and throw back.'

Her efforts at lightening the mood had failed. If anything his mood had become darker, the timbre of his voice dropping to an almost sinister whisper. She could see his jaw clench and unclench in her peripheral vision, and shivered at the sudden sapphire chill of his eyes.

She forced a smile to her lips, feeling strangely claustrophobic in the airy room, so close to his grim countenance. She was desperate to lighten the situation. Her body had relaxed and she deliberately straightened, pulling away from the mesmerising magnetism of his presence.

'I thought all good Greek boys wanted to settle down and have lots of little Greek babies? Little boys to carry on the family name?'

Alex had seen the wariness creep into her gaze, and gave a sudden laugh to ease the tension. Isobella was right. His mother nagged him constantly about him being the only chance to carry on the Zaphirides name. How ecstatic she'd been all those years ago, when Sonya had been on the scene. Her firstborn son settling down with a nice Greek girl.

He dipped Isobella quickly, and smiled down into her startled face as she clutched at his shoulders. 'What makes you think I'm a good Greek boy?' He pulled her up again just as quickly, and smiled at the sudden rag-doll feel to her frame, taking full advantage to pull her closer.

Isobella's head spun. His husky question had caused a wild leap in her pulse. His cerulean gaze was full of daring. His body was pressed into hers, and suddenly she was thinking of things—bad things—that bad boys did. She had to get this back on track.

She laughed to cover the nervous gallop of her

heart. 'I'm sure even bad Greek boys want the same thing.'

Alex pondered it for a moment and then grinned at her. 'No. But I bet their mothers do.'

She laughed genuinely this time. His humour was just the antidote to the spiralling sexual attraction. He joined her, and his wicked dimples tightened her pelvic floor muscles as if he'd stroked her belly.

The music ended and she was grateful, stepping out of his arms and heading off the floor before she was tempted to stay for another. One dance with catch-kiss-and-throw-back Alex was more than enough for her sanity. Dancing in his arms had made her want things, inappropriate things, and she had absolutely no intention of ever becoming hooked on Alexander Zaphirides' line.

Saturday and Sunday flew by for Isobella. There were several panels and workshops that she found very useful, and they had the added advantage of allowing her to hide from Alex. Not that he seemed interested in keeping an eye on her. She'd seen him on more than one occasion with Sonya following closely behind, and she knew that they'd met for drinks in the bar on Saturday night.

Maybe running into each other again had re-kindled old memories for Alex? Good ones as well. Maybe time had given him the distance he needed to be objective? Buffered the anger she had sensed in him while they had danced. Maybe he'd never really got over her? *Whatever.* He was a grown man and his personal life was none of her business.

She had sat in the audience and listened with rapt attention to his paper on Saturday—along with about every other woman in the room. His delivery had made somewhat hard statistical data eminently enticing, and she'd almost heard a collective whimper when he had finally finished.

His talk had been made all the more fascinating by the fact that for the first time since she'd met him he'd worn a tie. She'd got used to his open-necked style, and wouldn't have thought a tie could have improved on his potent sexuality. But she'd been wrong. He'd looked utterly professional—like the successful doctor-cum-businessman he was. He'd exuded all his usual confidence bordering on arrogance, but the tie had lent him an edge of power.

Sonya had certainly noticed it. Isobella had spotted her sitting cross-legged in a tight short skirt in the front row, circling her ankle lazily, flirting outrageously. She'd beamed up at the stage as if she owned him, and when everyone had clapped at the end she'd looked around, nodding at people as if she'd written the damn paper herself.

Isobella's paper had been well received, and she'd taken a full thirty minutes of questions, but she'd been disappointed that Alex hadn't made it. Her gaze had scanned the lecture theatre repeatedly, hoping to locate him. But the lights had been too bright in her eyes and she'd eventually given up and concentrated on her presentation.

So it had been a full two days, and as Isobella climbed out of the shower on Sunday night, enveloping herself in the luxury of the fluffy white gown, she was pleased they were over. There was a knock on the door, and her stomach growled in acknowledgement that her room service meal had arrived.

She tightened the belt around her waist, pulled the lapels together and bunched the gown around her throat, holding it in place as she opened the door. She'd treated herself to her favourite things from the menu, and her mouth was salivating in anticipation.

'Oh.' Isobella clutched the robe closer to her neck. Alex stood at her door. Even in her blurry without-glasses world she could make out that he was still wearing his black trousers and turquoise shirt from earlier that day, minus the jacket.

He gave her a look of enquiry. 'I've come at a bad time?'

Or a good one, as the case might be. He'd never seen her look so unclothed, even encased in towelling from neck to knee. The material was drawn tight around her body, showing off her slender build. Her hair was damp and her glasses were blissfully missing. She looked fresh-faced and rosy-cheeked. She looked very, very kissable.

'I'm sorry, I was expecting someone else,' she said, absently trying to calm the thrill of her pulse.

Alex bristled. She was opening the door dressed like this to someone else? 'Really?'

It was low and husky, but nothing disguised the note of displeasure in his voice. 'Room Service,' she said hastily, although quite why she felt the need to set the record straight she wasn't sure. If he could run around with his ex all weekend, who was he to say what she could do in the privacy of her hotel room? Bloody arrogant man.

Alex relaxed. The thought of her entertaining a man was disturbing, and he really didn't want to explore why. 'May I join you?'

Isobella gripped the door handle. 'No.'

Alex chuckled at her unflinching rejection. 'I hope you're having the prawns. They're divine.'

She nodded. 'And the beer-battered chips. And the sticky date pudding.'

Alex chuckled again. How did she manage to stay so slender? Every time he'd seen her this weekend she'd been stuffing her face with some calorie-laden morsel.

Isobella gripped the neckline of the gown harder. His laugh was sexy as hell. 'Is there something you want?' she asked. It came out a little harshly, but she was acutely aware that she was very undressed beneath her gown.

As she stood before him, showing off all her desirable womanly features for once, Alex could think of several things he wanted—very badly—but she was obviously annoyed at his intrusion. And he knew enough about her to know she just wasn't the catch-kiss-and-throw-back type.

He cleared his throat. 'Couple of things, actually. I thought I'd pop in and let you know your presentation was fantastic. You did a great job. Everyone's talking about it.'

Isobella frowned, finding the knowledge that he had been there after all disturbing. 'Thank you. I didn't know you'd caught it.'

He nodded. 'I was at the back.'

So he had been there, watching her in the darkened room. Her abdominal muscles clenched. She blinked to clear the sudden buzz in her head. 'There was something else?'

Alex nodded. 'I've just had a call from Cairns General hospital. A box jellyfish patient was admitted to their Intensive Care Unit a couple of hours ago. An eighteen-year-old female, an English tourist here on holiday.'

Isobella had no control over the gasp that escaped her lips, and was grateful that the door handle gave her something to hold on to. The pain that had scorched her body sixteen years ago haunted her in a blinding flash, stealing her breath. 'Is she okay?'

Alex heard the anguish in Isobella's voice and noticed the pinkness leech from her cheeks. He took a step towards her, concerned at her unexpected reaction. 'She's stable. She didn't have too much tentacular exposure. It wrapped itself around her thigh. She's having the antivenin and will go to the ward tomorrow, all going well.'

Isobella felt relief sweep her body at the good news. Still, she was rattled by the rekindled memories. 'Good,' she said weakly. 'That's good.'

'I told the consultant we'd call by in the morning and see her, before she's moved.'

Isobella's heart banged against her ribs in slow, explosive thuds. 'In Intensive Care?'

Alex frowned, bothered by the hint of reluctance he heard in her tone. 'That's okay, isn't it? We're going to be there anyway for the clinic. We can get a case history and take some photos.'

The thought of talking with a young woman who had been through what she'd been through was unsettling. In fact she wasn't looking forward to the clinic tomorrow at all. Even sixteen years later she wasn't sure she was ready to face other people's demons. She'd spent all this time hiding her scars from the world—how did these people voluntarily agree to expose themselves? She felt like a hypocrite. But, frankly, the thought of venturing into Intensive Care again was utterly terrifying.

'Isobella?'

She shut her eyes as the gravelly timbre of his

voice hardened her nipples, causing them to rub erotically against the fabric of her gown. Damn Alexander Zaphirides! Why hadn't he just left her in the lab? She tightened her grip on the door handle. 'Sure. No problem.'

'Pardon me, sir?'

Alex turned to find an impeccably dressed waiter standing behind him, a room service cart complete with starched linen at his side. 'Your feast.' He gestured to her as he stood aside to let the waiter pass.

Isobella's gaze followed the path of the trolley, laden with sophisticated silver domed plates, delicious smells wafting in its wake. She glanced back at Alex, the bearer of bad news.

Suddenly her appetite had completely deserted her.

Great! She was going to starve to death around this man.

CHAPTER FIVE

ALEX and Isobella waited outside the closed swing doors the next morning. She darted a nervous glance towards him and adjusted her glasses. He seemed so calm. Her heart was belting along in her chest like a runaway train, but he looked as poised as ever.

'Doesn't this bother you?' Nausea was roiling through her gut, and she needed to distract herself from it's vice-like grip.

Alex frowned. Isobella looked as pale this morning as she had last night. 'What?'

Isobella made an impatient noise in the back of her throat. The man had a trachey scar; he had to have spent some time in an ICU. 'Being back in Intensive Care. Won't it bring back some unpleasant memories for you?'

He shrugged. 'I don't really remember anything of the time I spent in Intensive Care. I was only in it for a few days, and the drugs pretty much made the whole time there a bit of a blur.'

Yes. Her memory was hazy too. But a mish-mash of distorted soundbites and snippets of fog-enshrouded images still occasionally woke her from her sleep at night. 'Probably just as well,' she said. 'Intensive Care's no Club Med.'

Alex raised an eyebrow. 'Oh?' There was a vehemence in her voice that sounded as if it came from personal experience.

Isobella tensed. 'I did a rotation there in my grad year,' she lied, amazed at how easily it slipped off her tongue. But she shouldn't be. Hadn't she been lying by omission to everyone for years, hiding from her past?

'Trust me, being in hospital at all is no Club Med.'

Isobella glanced up as the bleak truth in his gravelled tone swept to her very core. *Ain't that the truth?*

Then the doors opened and they were ushered inside, and Isobella's heartbeat picked up to a crazy canter.

The first thing that registered was the smell. It was that hospital smell. The same smell they all had, no matter where you were in the world.

Disinfectant and industrial-strength soap, mingling with floor wax and air deodorisers. Her nose wrinkled, and she realized it was one of the things she didn't miss about being a nurse.

And then the noises took over. Mechanical clatters. Monitor alarms trilling. Suction units slurping. A range of machines and pumps all blaring, attracting attention. A special ventilator called an oscillator, its membrane thumping at three hundred a minute, sounded like a pimped up car vibrating with too much bass. At one bed a woman was sobbing, at another a nurse was talking loudly to her patient while she restrained his flailing arms and called for assistance.

Isobella's eyes darted from bed to bed. The noises reverberated around the walls and ricocheted across her nerves. She felt like a cat on a hot tin roof. Somewhere the peal of a bedside buzzer splintered her tenuous hold on normality, and she lurched into Alex, clutching his arm.

Alex looked down at her, one dark brow winged in enquiry. 'You okay?'

She nodded, taking a few calming breaths as the spike in her pulse settled. 'Noisy places,' she murmured.

They spoke briefly with the consultant, who

confirmed that a skin scraping had been taken and sent to the Zaphirides lab in Brisbane. Isobella wished she was there, peering at it through her microscope, instead of here about to witness the damage it had wreaked.

They read through the chart, paying particular attention to the ambulance transport sheet at the front of the notes. Or at least Alex did. Isobella didn't read that the patient had been given an intramuscular injection of antivenin, or that she'd had just under a metre tentacle contact length. She was trying to find some Zen amidst her freaked-out state. Trying to tune out the noises and the smells and the memories to concentrate on the project.

The consultant personally directed them to the bed, introduced Danielle Cartwright and left them to it. The patient was wired up to a monitor, an oximeter peg attached to her finger. Even twelve hours post envenomation the English girl looked scared witless.

'I was wondering if we could ask you some questions, Danielle?' Alex asked, pulling up a chair beside the bed. Isobella stood on the opposite side.

The patient looked from one to the other and

nodded. 'It was so stupid. They told us when we first arrived at the hotel it was stinger season, but the water looked so inviting. I was just going in for a dip. To cool off. I mean…how unlucky can you be? I can't believe it. I still can't believe it.'

Isobella nodded, understanding the girl's dazed demeanour—box jellyfish stings were rare. It hadn't even crossed her own mind, wading into the water off Cardwell for the shoot that day, that she'd be a *Fleckeri* statistic.

'Can you tell us all you can remember from yesterday?'

'Like what?'

Alex smiled at her. 'Everything—from just before you went into the water until you got stung and what happened after.'

Isobella watched as Danielle responded to the calm tones of Alex's gentle enquiry. He was sitting forward in his chair, his elbows propped against his knees, his attention completely focused on his patient. As if Danielle Cartwright and her story were the most important things in his life.

Danielle responded beautifully, hesitantly at first, and then more surely as Alex's intense nods and murmurs and succinct questions garnered the information they needed. Isobella wondered, as she jotted down notes for when she was cataloguing the specimen on her return, if this was Alexander Zaphirides the surgeon she was seeing.

His bedside manner was superb—not something one generally learned from peering down a microscope or schmoozing at symposiums. Danielle trusted him—she could tell. He had already built a quick rapport. Had he been that kind of surgeon? The kind who took their time to explain and understand their patient's fears and worries? Had his patients adored him? Or had he been distant? Arrogant? Like the brief impression she'd had of him at the cocktail party?

Danielle faltered, and Isobella tuned back into the conversation.

'It was awful.' Danielle shuddered. She looked down at her hands, that were plucking at the sheet. 'The pain is...indescribable. It was like...like someone had taken a blowtorch to my leg, but it...it...'

Isobella took a step closer to the bed as the young woman struggled to adequately describe the unimaginable pain she'd experienced. Danielle's eyes had filled with tears, and she had a look of such abject terror on her face Isobella felt her stomach flop. She didn't have to ask to know that Danielle was back in the water again, reliving the dreadful moment.

'It was everywhere. It was in my head and my heart and my lungs. I couldn't breathe… I couldn't move…'

Danielle choked on a sob, and Isobella took another step closer and reached for the girl's fidgeting hand. Danielle looked startled at the intimacy as a tear trekked down her face. But she gripped Isobella's hand hard and gave her a tight, watery smile.

'And now I have this.' She peeled back the sheet to reveal the three livid purple lashes seared into the flesh of her left lower thigh. 'Look at it,' she gasped. 'It's horrible— hideous. I'm never going to be able to wear shorts again!'

Isobella leaned hard into the side of the bed as the *Fleckeri* damage leapt out at her. Danielle's emotions were so raw, evoking a hundred memories of a time she only wanted to forget. Isobella knew that plenty of people would tell Danielle how lucky she was—and, yes, she was—but Isobella also knew that living with a permanent unwanted tattoo was hard on the self-esteem and worse on the psyche. You felt branded. Unattractive. Unfemale. Unworthy.

The girl wouldn't get *such* banal platitudes from her.

Isobella squeezed Danielle's hand. 'It's hard now. But it gets easier.'

Alex frowned at the sight before him. *What the...?* He could see the white of Isobella's knuckles as she held Danielle's hand, and the now familiar molasses gaze was coating the young woman in compassion. He'd never seen Isobella looking so intense—not even in the few days he'd spent with her at the lab. He wouldn't have thought that possible.

'Isobella's right, Danielle,' Alex said quietly, dragging his gaze from Isobella's face. 'The scars lessen over time.'

That hadn't been what Isobella meant, but who wouldn't believe Alex when he was looking so self-assured, with his husky voice ringing with truth?

Danielle gulped and nodded her head, removing her hand from Isobella's and scrubbing at her face.

'Let me tell you about our project,' Alex said gently. 'I think you'll find it interesting.'

Danielle listened intently. The timbre and the flow of his voice were hypnotic, and his passion about his subject was not remotely blunted by the burred resonance.

'We'd like to enrol you in the study. We'd need to take some pictures of the wound and arrange for regular follow-ups after you go back to England. Isobella will look into that. We brought some information for you to read through.'

Alex glanced at her, and it took a second or two for Isobella to realise that he was waiting for her to hand over the literature. She blinked, and then delved around in her bag for the booklet.

'Here,' she said, smiling at Danielle. The young woman took the booklet from her and leafed through it. Isobella could see the information was going to be too much to take in right now. 'I'll be in touch, and we can go over any questions you might have. But do you mind if I take a few pictures of the lesions now for my database?' Isobella asked.

Danielle nodded. 'Okay.'

Isobella smiled her thanks and quickly snapped a dozen shots with the lab's high-resolution digital camera. The severe linear erythematous weals had a white ischaemic centre in what was known as a frosted ladder pattern. An acute inflammatory response had developed, causing some surrounding tissue oedema.

Isobella made sure she had some detailed angles. The researcher in her wanted to pore over the wound, discuss it with Alex in depth, but she didn't want to make Danielle too self-conscious. She knew she could inspect the photos in depth at a later date.

Danielle thanked them for coming and promised to read the literature. Alex stopped to write on the chart, but Isobella didn't want to stick around, and offered to go and buy them some coffee, arranging to meet Alex in the café in fifteen minutes.

It wasn't till she left the unit that Isobella felt as if she could breathe properly again, and her hand trembled as she thought about the anguish in Danielle Cartwright's voice. And this was just the beginning. Today would be fraught with hard-to-listen-to stories. Stories that would take her back to her own horrid experience. She yearned for the safety of her white coat and her microscope, nearly two thousand kilometres away in Brisbane.

'So where are these rooms the hospital have loaned us?'

Alex's low question vibrated near her ear and slithered down her arms, startling her. Had it not been for the lid she would have spilled his coffee everywhere. 'On the third floor,' she said stiffly, handing him the paper mug. 'We should get going too. Our first client arrives in fifteen minutes.'

Alex nodded at Little-Miss-Efficient who stood before him. She wasn't meeting his eyes, and he suspected that she'd been more affected by Danielle then she let on. She'd certainly been marvellously empathetic with the young woman.

They made their way in silence to the lifts. 'I think she'll be okay,' Alex said as the doors closed.

Isobella frowned. 'Sorry?'

'Danielle Cartwright.'

Her frown deepened. 'Maybe. Eventually.' Isobella had the feeling that the English tourist had some way to go.

'She's shaken at the moment, but the scarring is minimal,' Alex pointed out.

Isobella felt a surge of bile rise inside her at his casual dismissal. 'Not to her it isn't,' she said acidly.

The lift pinged and they disembarked. Alex wasn't sure what he'd said, but he'd obviously annoyed her. 'All I'm saying is that in the grand scheme of things she got off lightly.'

Isobella halted. 'She's an eighteen-year-old woman. A girl, really. Complete with all the screwed-up body images we all have from living in an airbrushed world. Her body has been physically marked. It's changed. She's confronting big issues and questioning her attractiveness to the opposite sex.'

Alex frowned down at her. Isobella was positively animated. Her eyes glittered, her cheeks were flushed and her chest heaved. He wasn't sure what was going on here, but he liked seeing her so alive. 'Men don't care about things like that.'

Isobella snorted. *Right.* She had first-hand experience of just how much men cared about disfiguring scars. 'It's all right for you, Mr Show-my-scars-off-to-the-world. It's easier for men. For some reason women find scars fascinating on a man—a turn-on. They make us want to take men home and feed the poor wounded heroes chicken soup while we kiss them better.'

Alex grinned down at her. 'Scars are a turn-on?'

Isobella gave a frustrated growl at the back of her throat and turned away, steaming ahead again, ignoring his husky chuckle. He was being deliberately inflammatory and she wasn't going to be his entertainment for the day. It was going to be harrowing enough.

'I just meant,' Alex said, following her into a large office area, 'that any man—any real man—wouldn't be turned off by scarring.'

'Well, don't mind me if my opinion of your sex is somewhat lower. I think you'd be amazed at what spooks men.'

Alex looked down at her speculatively. Some man had definitely done a number on her. 'Maybe you're hanging out with the wrong type of man?'

Isobella swallowed at the sinful quiver to his voice. Had it lowered a notch further?

'Look, Alex,' she said, determined not to open a conversation about her type of man, 'all I'm saying is Danielle's not an older woman who has already found her place in the world, has a career and kids and a husband, and is secure in herself. She's a teenager who still very much judges herself on what others think. Peer groups are vital at that age. Any little blemish can be devastating. A pimple can cause a meltdown at that age, for crying out loud!'

'You seem to know a lot about it.'

She shrugged as her heart pounded in her

chest. Had she given too much away? 'I was young once.'

And beautiful.

Alex found it hard to believe, in her unflattering clothes and grandma glasses, that Isobella had ever been a teenager. He drained his coffee. 'Well, let's find us a cure, then.'

Isobella had scheduled appointments every half-hour, so they wouldn't be rushed, but even so it would be a full day. Only six of the group actually lived in Cairns. The study had paid the expenses for the remainder, who lived in the far North Queensland region, to come to the clinic for the day.

There were four children between the ages of six and fourteen, and the rest were a cross section of adults from different backgrounds, cultures and socio-economic brackets. But their stories were all quite similar. An innocent swim in balmy tropical waters gone horribly wrong.

Isobella set up her laptop and appointed herself official scribe, determined to distance herself from the patients and the emotional impact of the information as much as possible. Alex could do all the talking and photo-taking while Isobella got the info down without involving herself in the stories.

But of course it didn't work out that way. Alex drew her in to every consultation, insisting she look at and give opinions on the scarring. He got her to talk about the project from her perspective, and it was impossible not to get involved. Not to put faces to people that until now had been just case numbers, distant voices over the phone.

Which was exactly what she'd hoped to avoid. Every person reliving their experiences, showing their scars, made her relive hers, tearing open the wounds a little further. Damn it, Reg was supposed to be here doing this. Her job had been to set it all up, not to participate. That was what she did—she co-ordinated the project from Brisbane and worked in the lab. Hers was not a field job. She'd never have applied for it had she known she'd be anywhere but in the safe haven of her lab.

Between patients she downloaded the digital shots and filed them, electronically attaching them to the case histories she'd taken, ignoring Alex. She told him it was an efficient use of her time and ducked his attempts at conversation. But in reality the things she was hearing were cutting deeply into her emotional barriers and she felt raw and exposed. She didn't need his razor-sharp analysis or unnerving scrutiny. And, frankly, she didn't trust the steadiness of her own voice.

Their last client for the day was forty-year-old Alice Spalding. She had twenty-year-old abdominal scarring from a *Fleckeri* and was the one patient Isobella had been dreading, being closest to her in nature.

Alice had brought her eight-month-old baby girl, Phoebe, with her, and Isobella's concerns disappeared as her heart just about melted. The baby had her mother's colouring—milky skin, with a crop of russet curls framing a cherubic face. Little fat arms and legs and huge round green eyes completed the irresistible package. How often had Isobella dreamed of having her own little one?

'I hope you don't mind,' Alice murmured. 'I'm still feeding her, so I had to bring her to Cairns with me.'

'Of course not,' Alex dismissed, ushering them both in.

Isobella watched as Phoebe gave Alex a gooey smile and he wiggled his eyebrows at her. The baby giggled and Alex did it again. *Yeah, kid, he's something else, isn't he?*

'You look like you're an old hand, Dr Zaphirides,' Alice commented.

'Number one favourite uncle, that's me.' He grinned.

Isobella didn't scribe a thing during the consultation, too mesmerised by Phoebe. Or at least by the way Alex was with her. He spoke to Alice while automatically picking up all the objects Phoebe had taken from her mother's hand, sucked once and then thrown on the floor. He was amazingly patient, and Isobella felt her attraction for him treble.

'We just need to have a look at your old scars and photograph them,' he said to Alice. 'Come on, madam.' Alex clapped his hands and plucked the baby off her mother's lap, holding her against his chest.

Phoebe looked very small against his largeness, and Isobella found herself wondering again what a child of his would look like. Dark curls. Olive skin. Blue eyes like Alex's that spoke of Greece and the sea and all its secrets.

Alex dropped a kiss on the mop of hair. 'You can go to Isobella.'

Isobella blinked. 'What?'

He passed the baby over, amused at the look of consternation on her face. But she did hold out her arms, even if her eyes were wide beneath her ridiculous glasses. 'It's just for a minute,' he murmured.

Phoebe landed in her arms, and Isobella caught her close in an automatic response, surprised at the weight of the little girl. She settled Phoebe on her hip and looked down at the earnest, chubby-cheeked angel. Phoebe stared at her solemnly for a few moments, a small frown on her face, and then reached for Isobella's glasses.

'Oh!' Isobella said as Phoebe managed to remove them easily and everything went blurry.

'Out of the mouths of babes...' Alex said, already liking the improvement.

'I can't see a thing without them,' Isobella objected as she rescued the glasses from receiving a baby saliva bath. She placed them back, high on her nose, and was relieved when Phoebe found a different distraction in the buttons on her high-necked blouse.

'Okay, Alice, let's have a look,' Alex said, reluctantly dragging his gaze back to the matter at hand. Isobella looked good with a baby on her hip. Too good.

Alice lay down on the examination couch and pulled up her T-shirt. Two long tentacular marks branded her abdomen. They had faded a little, lost their livid quality, but they were still stark against Alice's pale skin.

Alex snapped some pictures. 'Did you have any problems conceiving?'

Isobella, who'd been swaying gently, suddenly stopped. She looked at Alice's abdominal scarring and shivered—it was nasty, but nowhere near as nasty as hers. What did Alex know about *Fleckeri* stings and fertility?

Alice nodded. 'Why else would I have a baby at forty?'

Alex chuckled. 'Good point.'

'The docs told me when it first happened that they didn't know if it would affect my fertility, given the area of the scarring and the unknown long-term side effects of the antivenin. Ever since the sting I've had erratic periods, and we tried for years to fall pregnant—had all the tests and everything checked out normally. The gynae guys were reluctant to officially say it, but unofficially they think the sting to my abdomen somehow affected my reproductive organs. We'd given up years ago. Little Phoebe was our surprise package.'

Isobella hugged the child closer as Alice's story chilled her to the bone. The specialists had said the same thing to her. They didn't know the long-term effects of such extensive envenoma-tion to the abdomen. They didn't know the long-term side effects of six doses of antivenin. And at nineteen, with more immediate things to worry about, it hadn't been a big issue for her. But the older she got, the more it weighed on her mind.

She too had been plagued with erratic periods since the sting. Had gone from regular as clock-work to all over the shop. Had that fateful day sixteen years ago robbed her of her fertility? As well as her lover and her self-esteem? What if she could never have a baby?

Phoebe squirmed and she hushed her, rubbing her chin against the baby's forehead, inhaling her sweet smell. She wanted a baby more fiercely in this moment then she'd thought was possible—so fiercely her womb ached. Damn Alexander Zaphirides. Nothing had been the same since he'd walked into her lab.

Alex turned away while Alice fixed herself up,

and his gaze fell on Isobella. Phoebe was fidgeting, and he noticed the tension in Isobella's knuckles as she held the baby tight. Isobella's eyes were closed, her forehead against Phoebe's, as if the baby were the most precious piece of cargo in the world. She certainly didn't look as if she was about to let the child go any time soon.

Isobella opened her eyes as Phoebe protested against the firm hold. Alex's cerulean gaze greeted her and held her captive. She could feel it probing, his blue eyes stripping away her glasses, her thoughts, her defences. Holding Phoebe had left her vulnerable, too weak to shut herself off to his intuitive gaze. What would it be like to hold Alex's baby, their baby, in her arms?

Alex's breath stopped in his chest. She was so still, the guardedness in her eyes missing for once. She was looking at him, her gaze thick with yearning. And he wasn't entirely sure it had to do with Phoebe. There was something more in her molasses eyes. Something that spoke to him, that tightened his groin, that danced along the muscles of his lower abdomen. He took a step towards her.

'I guess I'd better get her back to the hotel. It's nearly time for bed,' Alice said.

Isobella tore her gaze from Alex's and snatched a last whiff of Phoebe's sweet, sweet smell before she handed her over.

'Thanks for coming in today,' Alex said, aware of Isobella busying herself at the laptop, attaching the digital camera.

Alice left, and nothing could be heard in the room but the sound of Isobella's fingers flying over the keys. Alex looked down at her, trying to fathom what he'd seen in her face, what the hell had just passed between them.

'You looked good with a baby,' he murmured, his voice huskier than usual.

Isobella's fingers stumbled against the keys for a second as her heart accelerated madly. 'Everyone looks good with a baby,' she said, eyes firmly on her laptop screen, refusing to be drawn.

'Join me at the Terrace Bar for a drink?' Alex requested as they walked into the hotel foyer. The taxi ride from the hospital had been accomplished in silence, with Isobella staring out the window.

'No,' Isobella said. She didn't want to socialise with him. The day had been an enormous strain, and she wanted to soak in a tub and get an early night for their crack-of-dawn start tomorrow.

'Don't be difficult, Isobella.' Alex had toler-ated her silence in the cab, but he would not put up with her mood for the next few days. 'If it makes it easier, consider it an order.'

Isobella gritted her teeth. His tone left her in no doubt he thought she was being a petulant child. Not the consummate professional he demanded her to be. She had a good mind to tell him to shove his job. This wasn't what she'd signed on for.

Just three more days. That's all.

Why blow the best job she'd ever had in a fit of feminine pique? She squared her shoulders. 'Yes, sir.'

Alex gave her back a small smile as he followed her brisk strides into the bar. He stopped to order drinks, watching her weave her way through the late-afternoon patrons. He followed her a few minutes later.

He stopped at the entry to the large terracotta terrace that jutted out over the beach, searching for her blonde head. He located her easily, propped against the stainless steel railing, staring out to sea. The sunset blazing low on the horizon gilded her hair, giving the impression of a halo, and he gave a wry smile.

The tangerine blush of the sky grew larger as he approached, like a giant canvas. The colours of the setting sun bled from a pale blush to pomegranate to crimson. The steady rhythm of the nearby waves calmly lapped at the all-but-deserted beach.

And despite the glorious sunset, and the array of beautiful people there to witness it, and her dreadful sense of style, she was still the most interesting thing on the balcony.

'Hard to believe that cyclone's still hanging around,' he said, nudging her arm with a frosty cocktail glass.

Isobella shivered as his voice brushed the skin near her ear. 'I heard it was heading back to sea,' she said, clutching the rail for a moment before turning side on and taking the proffered umbrellaed glass. 'What is it?' she asked dubiously.

'Sex on the Beach.' He smiled.

Isobella took a second to steady herself, gripping the glass. 'I'm celibate these days, Dr Zaphirides,' she said dropping it on a nearby table and not caring that it probably cost him an arm and a leg.

Alex chuckled. 'That's a shame. Celibacy is not good for you.'

'Spoken like a true man,' she said derisively.

Alex chuckled again, but turned to face the water taking a swig of his long-necked beer. She watched his profile, fascinated by the way the light sea breeze ruffled his luxurious locks, brushing them against his forehead.

'What do you want, Alex?'

Alex took a moment to absorb the peace and the quiet resilience of the ocean before he turned to the harnessed civility of her face. 'You were great today.'

Isobella gave him a dubious look. 'I prefer my microscope.'

'I don't think you do.'

The accuracy of his husky observation rankled. Particularly as he was right. The patient contact today had been challenging, and she'd kept herself as distant as possible, but she'd been surprised to find herself being drawn into it again. She looked away from the piercing insight of his gaze, watching the to and fro of the ocean.

'Why are you locking yourself way in the lab? You built fabulous rapports with Phoebe and our clients. You were great with Danielle. You were just what that poor frightened girl needed. You were a nurse today.'

Isobella shrugged. What did it matter? She wasn't a nurse any more. 'Old habits die hard.'

'You'd make a great field officer.'

She turned to face him again, his open-neck shirt reminding her that despite his flattery they were too different. 'I don't want to be a field officer.'

'You gave up because you got too close to your patients, didn't you? It was nothing to do with wanting a change. I saw how you were with Danielle. Your empathy was palpable. Did it get too much? Did you have a breakdown?' It would explain her jumpiness this morning in the ICU.

Isobella didn't answer. Not even to tell him he was way off base. Let him think what he liked. It was none of his damn business.

'Don't you miss it?'

Isobella sighed. 'Do you miss surgery?'

Alex shook his head. 'Before the cancer I was set on the glamour of surgery. Plastics. Burns, particularly. To me there was no other kind of medicine, no other kind of doctor. Why become a doctor if you couldn't be a surgeon?'

He looked at her for confirmation and she nodded, not wanting to break his dialogue, mesmerised by his animated face, the gravel in his voice and the poetry of the ocean.

'Then I was forced to take time away. Get on the other side of the bed for a change. The unglamorous side. And all around me was this whole other medical world that existed outside of the operating theatre. It didn't take me too long to realise that if you took my scalpel away I was still a doctor. I could still help people.'

Isobella nodded. She understood. It was what she was trying to do after all. Help people. People who depended on what she was doing. People like her. It was just that she preferred the anonymity of the white coat.

'It's no different for me. This is the way I choose to help people now.'

'But you have a gift. You said just the right things to Danielle today. You're wasted in the lab.'

She looked into his earnest gaze. 'I'm a woman, Alex. I have female intuition. That's all it was.'

Yes, she was a woman. And a very original woman at that. With a body she hid in baggy clothes and a face she camouflaged behind truly hideous glasses. Why on earth did he want her so much?

'Have dinner with me tonight.'

Isobella was tempted. The man looked utterly devastating, and his gravelly invitation was laced with a sinful edge. The female inside that she'd tamed and caged, strait-jacketed in an asexual shell, wanted to indulge and to hell with the consequences. But her mental scars, and the memory of Anthony's face filled with revulsion, held her back.

She turned away looking to the activity on the terrace, desperate for the noise and buzz to cover her confusion in place of the tranquility of the waves.

And Sonya was there, striding towards them in a little black dress, red heels and a flower in her lush long hair. She had a wide smile on her scarlet lips and a look of possession that gave Isobella the perfect retreat.

'I think your dance card's full,' she murmured, pushing away from the railing.

Alex watched as Isobella departed, brushing past Sonya and nodding a slight greeting.

She didn't look back.

CHAPTER SIX

ISOBELLA was pleased to be on terra firma, even if the sand was being eroded from beneath her feet with each lap of the waves. Alex had been right. Piccolo Island had been worth the rigours of the trip—they'd landed in Eden.

A two-hour small plane trip from Cairns to Temora Island and then another hour's boat ride had not been good for her equilibrium. Seeing Alex in boardies that clung to his bottom and showed off a fair portion of exquisitely sculpted dark-haired calf and thigh muscle hadn't been great for it either. But his casual T-shirt, exposing the bronzed column of his neck and the corded strength of his arms, had thankfully been enough to keep her mind off the endless ocean.

She looked around. Even at nine in the morning the bone-white sand was warm beneath her toes on the sun-drenched beach as they walked towards the main buildings visible through some foliage. The sun caressed her skin and danced beams on the crystal blue water in a dazzling kaleidoscope of light, causing Isobella's pupils to constrict in protest. She donned her owlish prescription sunglasses and was grateful for the broad brim of her hat.

A wiry-looking man with a woolly beard, an un-buttoned shirt flapping in the breeze and a toddler on his hip strode purposefully towards them. 'Dr Zaphirides, great to have you here again.'

'Mike,' Alex said warmly, extending his hand to Dr Mike Caldwell who ran the Piccolo Research Station with his wife, Dr Theresa Crane. They were both marine biologists, conducting a range of experiments within the Great Barrier Reef marine park and beyond. 'Knock it off with the Dr Zaphirides.'

Mike laughed. 'Sure thing, Alex. And who do we have here?'

Alex introduced Isobella, explaining about Reg's last-minute withdrawal, and then turned his attention to Mike's two-year-old, giving the boy's hair a ruffle. 'I can't believe how much Sam's grown. He was just a baby when I was here last.'

Sam reached his arms out to Alex, and Alex

plucked the toddler out of his father's arms and grinned down at him.

'Well, he's into everything now. A right little monkey—aren't you, mate?'

Isobella was grateful for the tinted glasses as she watched Alex beam indulgently at the angelic-looking child with the wild gleam in his eyes. He looked as comfortable holding Sam as he had on the boat and as he had at the symposium. Nothing seemed to throw him. He held the child confidently, chatting with Mike while still paying attention to Sam.

'Where's Theresa?'

'She's gone out with Ruth, one of the students, to check on some of the stinger traps.'

Isobella felt her heartbeat accelerate, excited and terrified in equal measure to see what Theresa brought back with her. She wondered how far out they had to go to set the traps, as box jellyfish didn't inhabit the waters around the reefs.

'They'll be back some time in the afternoon,' Mike continued. 'I'm on Sam duty today.'

'Sam,' Sam said.

Alex chuckled. 'Is that you?'

'Sam,' the child repeated, obviously proud of himself.

'Come on—I'll show you where to stash your stuff,' Mike said.

Isobella followed the two men up a sandy path through some scrubby vegetation. Alex was still holding Sam, and she wondered what kind of alternative universe she'd entered. Damn it. It was easier to distance herself from Alex in the lab. This whole tropical island thing was too… casual. She longed for the formality of the cold sterile lab and her white coat.

The research station consisted of several structures. Two concrete buildings fronted the cleared area, their roofs covered in solar panels. A decent-sized satellite dish protruded from the one set a little further back. Mike took them into the closest one, which was obviously the living quarters.

A small anteroom where various pieces of snorkeling equipment were stored opened into very basic living quarters, consisting only of a hallway from which three bedrooms and a bathroom ran off. Woven seagrass matting covered the concrete floor.

'I'm sorry—this is it,' Mike apologized, as he opened the door to a small room with bunk beds pushed against the far wall. An old desk and some wall-mounted shelves above a low chest of drawers were the only other furniture in the room. 'I didn't think it would be a problem with you and Reg. Ruth and Kate share the end room, and Theresa, Sam and I are in the other.'

Isobella surveyed the basic room, the implication that she would be sharing it with Alex sinking into her consciousness like the proverbial stone. *Great*. How would she sleep with him so near? She'd been cultivating distance in her relationships ever since Anthony's rejection. This was getting out of hand.

Alex saw Isobella's hand creep up to her throat. He'd noticed she did that whenever she was anxious about something. Her fingers stroked the polo neck nervously. For God's sake—he was hardly likely to jump her in the middle of the night.

He preferred his women willing, not looking like a Victorian heroine about to be ravished by a rake. And he was her boss—even if he had been thinking way too many inappropriate thoughts where Isobella was concerned. Already he was wondering what she wore to bed.

'Do you have any spare swags?' he asked Mike.

Distance—that was what he needed. Although

if her day clothes were anything to go by, her nightwear was probably neck to toe and fairly distance-provoking anyway.

'Sure. On the shelf.'

Alex nodded. 'I'll take mine down to the beach.'

The beach? As much as she didn't want him big and male and sleepy only meters away, she knew it was selfish to banish him to the outdoors. They were both adults, for goodness' sake, and it was only three nights.

'Alex.' Isobella turned to him in protest. 'Don't be silly. I'm sure we're capable of bunking together for a few nights.'

'I like the beach. You should try it one night. The waves lulling you to sleep and a blazing bonfire. Away from all the city lights the stars are amazing.'

'Full moon too for the next few nights,' Mike added.

Isobella conjured the picture in her mind. Her and Alex camped out under the stars together. There was an intimacy to it she shied from instantly. 'Thanks—I'm more the five-star type.'

Mike laughed. 'Well, it ain't the Ritz, but it's all we've got. Dump your bags in here for the moment anyway, and I'll show you around.'

They moved into the other besser block

building sporting the dish. There was nothing rudimentary about this one. High-tech was an understatement. Mike showed off his mini-lab with pride. State-of-the-art equipment covered every surface—the latest high-powered microscopes, computers, and a sophisticated communication centre complete with the latest in radio technology.

'Wow,' Isobella muttered, totally dazzled by the equipment. The lab was a compact version of her own workplace, and she doubted Mike and Theresa wanted for anything.

Mike laughed. 'Pretty impressive, huh?'

'I'll say.'

'We couldn't do it on government support alone. We rely on donations from private industry too. Zaphirides Medical Enterprises has been particularly generous.'

Mike walked them through the different experiments they were undertaking for a variety of organizations, both governmental and private. It seemed odd to be taking a tour through tech central with a barely dressed tour guide looking like a grizzly and toting a toddler on his hip.

They stopped by a large screen. 'This is our weather tracking station,' Mike said. 'It's a direct feed from the department of meteorology. Cyclone Mary's still hovering.' He pointed to the swirling, menacing mass of low pressure a few hundred kilometres away.

'Do you think she'll turn back towards us?' Alex asked.

Mike shrugged. 'Who knows? Meteorology think it'll keep heading out and fizzle. But you know women.' He dug Alex in the ribs. 'Pretty hard to predict.'

Alex laughed. *Wasn't that the truth?* A classic example was standing right next to him.

'Dare you to say that when Theresa is here.'

Mike hooted. 'Do I look stupid?'

Isobella ignored them. 'So everything's run on solar power?'

Mike nodded. 'We have a back-up generator, but we don't carry much fuel so we try only to use that in an emergency. We get enough sunshine to power the lab twenty-four-seven, and we try to conserve energy everywhere else.'

They wandered outside, and Mike gestured them over to the outdoor cooking area. 'We cook and eat here mostly,' he said. It was an open three-sided structure, with a cement slab floor, a thatched roof and a large table grounded into concrete.

A fancy gas barbecue that would have been at home in the gardens of Buckingham Palace dominated the back wall, along with a large camp fridge. A pantry of dry food supplies and cooking equipment completed the space.

'We take it in turns to cook. It's mine tonight,' Mike said.

'Do you get much fresh food, or is it mainly tinned and pre-packaged?' Isobella asked.

'We get our supplies from Temora once a fort-night. Kate brought back our latest when she went to pick up you guys. So the first week or so we have more fresh food, and we always have plenty of fresh fish. Theresa's throwing a line in while she's out today, so hopefully she'll catch a couple of nice reef fish for tonight.'

Mike showed them a locked storage shed next. It was set slightly apart from the rest of the build-ings and was about the size of two garden sheds, again securely cemented into the concrete slab.

'We keep all kinds of supplies in here. Gas bottles, torches, batteries, spare motor parts for the generator, fuel, all kind of bits and pieces to perform running repairs.'

'Looks like you have to be a jack-of-all-trades,' Isobella murmured.

'It helps.' Mike grinned. 'The shed, as with the rest of the buildings, is cyclone-rated. But I guess you don't really know until it's weathered one.'

'Let's hope Mary doesn't put that rating to the test in the next few days,' Alex interjected.

Isobella couldn't help but agree. 'What about all the lab supplies? Are they kept in here too?'

Mike shook his head, bending to place a fractious Sam on the sandy ground. 'The lab stuff's too expensive to risk out here. There's a purpose-built room at the back of the lab where all the supplies are stored.'

A little hand touched her leg, and Isobella almost jumped. She looked down to find Sam looking up at her, grinning. He had obviously been attracted to the large yellow flowers on her sarong. Her heart contracted at his easy smile. She reached down and tentatively touched his downy hair.

'Come on, Sam, let's show them the genny.'

Sam took his father's hand, and they followed Mike around the back of the shed to where the generator sat. 'It's here in case we need emergency power for some reason—if the solar goes down. It's wired in to support the essential areas of the lab—the fridges and computers mainly. I've only ever had to use it once, but I fire it up every week and do a maintenance check on it.'

'Isn't it noisy?' Isobella asked.

Mike shook his head. 'It has a silencer installed. It'd scare the feathers off the birds otherwise. Piccolo's bird population is protected.'

The tour over, Mike and Alex started talking about funding and Isobella left them to it. She went back to the bunkroom and riffled through her bag for the notebook she'd stashed in it. It proved elusive, so she emptied the contents over the bottom bunk, ignoring the dress she'd resolutely snubbed the last few days. Finally she located the spiral book and grabbed her laptop. If she must be stuck on paradise with the twin distractions of a gorgeous Greek and an adorable toddler—two things she wouldn't ever have—then she was going to need to completely absorb herself in work.

Alex passed her on her way out. 'Hey, wait for me. I'll just be a minute,' he said.

Alex entered the bunkroom, grabbing his digital underwater camera and a towel. He looked at the mess strewn over the bed beside his bag, surprised that the neat, methodical Isobella had left her belongings in such disarray. She must have been in a hurry.

His gaze fell on a scrap of silk and lace and his hands stilled.

Hello!

He looked a little closer. Several bra and knicker sets were lying on the top of the jumble of clothes. He could see two g-strings—one lacy and red, the other black satin with a leopard print trim and an intriguing bow. There was even a matching satin leopard print bra.

A cream-coloured bra edged with delicate lace and decorated with a small jewelled butterfly nestled in the cleavage was somehow even more inviting than the colourful numbers. It reminded Alex of her, of her personality—understated, quiet, demure—and it took all of his will-power not to touch.

His heart thudded in his chest. Under all those awful high-necked shirts and baggy pants, underneath her white coat, little Miss Don't-look-at-me had been harbouring scraps of lace and satin. If he'd been placing bets he would have backed sensible white cotton granny undies and functional bras.

He spied a gauzy lilac, completely see-through

negligee with three tiny buttons down the bodice—did she sleep in this? He groaned. How was he going to look at her again? Look at her clothes and not wonder what wisps of material were beneath? Ignoring her had been surprisingly difficult anyway, but this? It was as if he knew a secret about her. A delicious, wicked secret.

He took a couple of deep cleansing breaths and left the room. 'Well, I don't know about you,' Alex said when he found her outside staring at the ocean, forcing his voice to be normal, 'but I'm going in for a swim. Why don't you come?'

Isobella turned to face him, her eyes widening as she realised he'd taken his shirt off. She swallowed. His chest was magnificent, spattered with dark hair, thicker across his pecs and becoming sparser and narrower as it arrowed down his flat abdomen and disappeared behind his boardies. Dear God—with that voice and those abs she felt as if Lucifer himself was trying to lure her into the water.

The waves lapped the beach in perfect synchronicity with the beat of her heart. It was as if they were saying—*We dare you, we dare you, we dare you...*

She dragged her gaze away from his chest, ignoring the siren call of the ocean. As inviting as the water looked, and even if she had been able to wade into it without having a panic attack, there was no way she could go in with Alex. Not shirtless. At the moment not even if he'd been dressed in a three-piece suit. Her libido had just roared to life big-time.

'I…I didn't bring my togs.'

Alex thought about the black lace and leopard print set back in the room. That would make a great bikini. Why was she hiding her body? The sarong afforded him the fullest view he'd ever had of her legs, and if those calves and ankles were anything to go by then the rest of her legs were spectacular.

'You come to a gorgeous coral cay in the middle of the Great Barrier Reef and you don't bring your togs?'

Alex's muscles rippled as he talked, and the waves kept up their taunting rhythm. *Dare you, dare you, dare you.* 'I thought we were here to work,' she said testily.

He wondered what kind of underwear she had on right now. Lace? Satin? Silk? Red? Pink? Blue? Was she wearing a thong? *Oh, God.*

'We're here to observe. I'm sure no one minds if we take the odd dip to cool off or do a little snorkelling,' Alex said sardonically.

'I told you,' she said defensively. 'I'm not keen on the ocean. I prefer dry land.'

Which was true. If someone had a gun pointed to her head and told her to get in then she could do it. But while she had a choice she was staying dry.

Alex couldn't believe what he was hearing. It was hot, and the crystal waters beckoned irresistibly. He wanted to wrench the sunglasses off her face so he could see into her eyes. Hell, he wanted to strip her shirt off and see what she was wearing underneath. He placed his hands firmly on his hips lest they be tempted to act on their own volition.

'So you're just going to wander around an island paradise dressed from neck to knee for three days, like some nineteenth-century missionary?' The fact that she was one thing underneath while pretending to be another on the outside was driving him mad. 'Aren't you hot in that?' he asked out of sheer exasperation.

Isobella looked down at her attire. She'd donned the sarong this morning, knotted it high on her waist and teamed it with one of her many high-necked loose-fitting smock-type shirts that brushed her elbows. It was a far cry from her modelling days, but the sarong was cotton and allowed air flow. It was a little shorter than she'd have liked, but unfortunately her height often worked against her.

'It's sun smart,' she said frostily, piqued at his description of her fashion sense.

'So, let me guess?' he said scathingly, taking in her notebook and laptop. 'You're heading for the lab, right?'

Isobella gritted her teeth. 'You may look at this as a snorkelling junket, Dr Zaphirides, and that's fine—you're the boss. But I'm here to observe and learn and work. Yes, work,' she continued, as Alex opened his mouth to interject. 'I miss it. I'm sure there'd be others who would jump at the chance to frolic on a tropical island, but I enjoy my work. And I'm damn good at it. This project is important to me. And, quite frankly, I really resent that you've dragged me away from it.'

Alex looked down into the dark tint of her glasses. Did she really have nothing else in her life other than her damn white coat and her microscope? Maybe she hadn't been joking about the celibacy? So what was with the sexy under-wear? That didn't say celibate lab geek. It said I'm female and I love it.

'Lady, you need a hobby. All work and no play makes Isobella a dull girl.' And leopard print did not say dull.

Unfashionable and dull. Great. 'I don't exist to be interesting,' she snapped.

Alex winged an imperious eyebrow. 'Patently.'

Just as well he couldn't see the dark look hidden behind her equally dark glasses. Why was he being so bloody-minded about this? And why, why, despite his criticism, did his chest still draw her gaze and the waves still drum their primal rhythm? *Dare you, dare you, dare you.*

'Well, seeing as how you employ me, you should be grateful. Do you want an assistant with her head in her wardrobe or one who's dedi-cated to the important things?'

Right now he'd settle for the wardrobe. And a private fashion parade.

Grateful? He should be grateful? That she was determined to bury herself away in the name of his research project? How long had she been spinning herself this kind of claptrap? She didn't truly believe it, did she? Camouflaging her body and clinging to the cloistered world of a sterile lab in the name of science when obviously underneath there was a lot of suppressed sexuality? And if she thought he wouldn't go there because it was inappropriate, she was wrong.

'This isn't about work. This is about hiding. About running away. Now, I don't know what it is that you're running from, but don't pretend this is something that it's not.'

His gravelly words had nailed her motives to the wall, and she resented his searing insight. Her breath stuck in her throat and she forced it in and out, refusing to take his bait. To hell with him. 'Oh, and you're so well adjusted, Mr Catch-kiss-and-throw-back?'

Alex sucked in a breath. She had learned too much about him in such a short time, and he was treading dangerous waters. His gaze was drawn to the agitated rhythm of her chest beneath her shapeless blouse. If he didn't get away from her now he was going to say or do something he'd regret. Or at least something that could have him up in front of a sexual harassment tribunal.

'That's *Dr* Catch-kiss-and-throw-back to you,' he snapped, and then strode away and didn't stop until he was totally immersed in the tepid tropical water, wishing the research station was situated on an island off Antarctica instead.

Theresa and Ruth arrived back in the afternoon, and Isobella was excited to see their spoils. Two box jellyfish had been trapped, one fully grown. She suppressed a shudder at the savage beauty of one of the most feared, venomous creatures on the planet.

The marine stinger, almost transparent, floated in a giant container, its tentacles undulating gracefully with the rock of the water like a ballerina perfecting a pirouette. It looked harmless, almost pretty. Hard to believe it could kill in minutes.

She engrossed herself in the lab, helping Theresa and her two students with the preliminary experiments and inputting the data. Anything. Anything to keep her mind off Alex.

'Would you look at them?' Theresa laughed at one stage.

Distracted by the tentacular material she was studying under the microscope, Isobella muttered, 'Hmm?' as she looked up.

'Alex playing with Sam.'

Isobella heard a squeal and, despite not wanting it to, her gaze was drawn through the large glass window that afforded the lab area an almost one-eighty-degree view of the beach. Sam was naked in the late-afternoon light, and the sky was a vibrant array of purples and pinks as somewhere to the west of them the sun journeyed to the other side of the horizon. Alex was laughing, still shirtless, as he dug a sandcastle for the toddler.

'Mmm,' she said, feigning disinterest and returning her eyes to the microscope.

They dined on fresh snapper for tea, and Isobella was content to let the conversation swirl around her. The global warming research Mike and Theresa were also conducting was fascinating stuff, and Isobella realised she could have listened all night. But the sea air was working its magic, and by eight-thirty she was yawning.

'Well, that's me done for,' she said, standing. 'Think I'll hit the sack.'

Everyone protested except the one person she'd been studiously avoiding looking at all evening. But she'd been more than aware of Alex's intense Aegean gaze.

'I'll see you all in the morning.'

Island moonlight filtered through the un-adorned window in her room as Isobella stripped down to her lacy turquoise bra and knickers. Given that there was no electricity in the living quarters it was just as well. She pulled a V-necked singlet over her head that overlapped the band of her undies. She usually slept in the lilac negligee. That had been all right for Cairns, in her own suite, but here, with Alex so close by, she wanted to be more covered. She couldn't bear to wear one of her high-necked shirts all night, though, so the singlet was a good com-promise.

She'd made her bed earlier, and crawled into it now, bone-weary in a way she hadn't been for a long time. Sleep was often elusive for her, and she usually read journal articles and research papers she'd brought home late into the night. But not even her earlier confrontation with Alex was enough to stop her eyes from drooping. It must be the salt air and the rhythmic lullaby of the waves, or the soft kiss of moonbeams on her face, but as soon as her head hit the pillow she slept.

Alex tiptoed into the room an hour later to retrieve his swag, moonlight guiding the way. He'd told himself he wouldn't look at her, but as he turned from the shelving, swag in hand, his gaze fell on her sleeping face. She'd removed her glasses and, shadowed as it was, her features relaxed instead of alert and tense, she looked impossibly young.

He found his thoughts wandering to what lay beneath the sheet she'd pulled up to her chin. There was no way he could tell. But that didn't stop him thinking about which item out of her bag of goodies she was sleeping in tonight. He felt his groin tighten and sighed, flicking off the torch as he left the room. No way was he going to sleep tonight. In fact he might never sleep again, thinking of Isobella in that lilac negligee.

The next day dawned bright and clear again, and Isobella and Alex eagerly threw themselves into the routine of Piccolo. They were polite but cool to each other—professional. Rigidly adhering to their boss/subordinate roles. If the crew of Piccolo noticed, they didn't say anything, but Isobella swore she saw a raised eyebrow or two pass between Mike and Theresa.

Alex tried to talk her into going out on the boat with him and Mike, so she could witness the different stages of each experiment first hand, but she adamantly refused and he didn't push it. She was wrapped in another tent-like contraption today, but he swore it was more distracting than had she been walking around naked. The last thing he needed to be thinking about on the boat was the colour of her underwear.

So Isobella stayed with Theresa, Ruth and Kate, and had a thoroughly interesting day in the lab. She hadn't been lying to Alex—she did miss her job—so it was great to be back in a familiar environment, despite the dramatic difference in setting. She even took some time out and built a sandcastle with Sam.

The day flew by until the men came back, and then there was more lab work, and it was evening before she knew it. Once again it got to eight-thirty and the lure of bed beckoned. The fact that she'd barely seen or spoken to Alex all day made it all the more likely she'd sleep soundly.

Alex awoke on the beach the next morning to a very menacing-looking sky. Dark clouds had erased the sunshine, casting a grey shadow across suddenly choppy waters. It was windy, and he rose and went straight into the lab. Mike was sitting at the weather station.

'Mary?' Alex queried.

Mike nodded. 'She turned late last night. They've classed her as a category four at the moment. It's not going to hit us directly, but skirt around us. The beaurea have confirmed it should pass by about midnight tonight, on its way to hit an isolated spot on the far North Queensland coast. It's going to be a rough night, though.' He turned to Alex. 'Bloody women, huh?'

Alex grinned. 'I suppose it's too late to evacuate to Temora?'

Mike nodded ruefully. 'Bad swells. Strong wind warning for coastal shipping. Not recommended. We're going to have to wait it out here.'

Alex rubbed at his morning stubble. 'Batten down the hatches?'

'You got it.'

And that was what they did. All day. Everyone pitched in. Everything was secured. The very last thing they needed was flying debris smashing into the precious and very expensive solar panels. Glass was reinforced with tape. Some of the taller trees were trimmed. The satellite dish was lashed to the roof to reinforce it.

First aid equipment and other supplies like batteries, food, torches and water were hoarded in the living quarters. An old CB radio Piccolo had used before the more sophisticated communications centre had been installed in the lab was set up in Mike and Theresa's room so they could get updates on the cyclones progress and have it handy in case of an emergency.

The boat, already tossing in the turbulent sea, was secured against the sturdy girders of the wooden jetty, while everything that could become a projectile was removed from it.

The security of the lab was paramount to them all, and they worked to make sure that everything was locked down inside and that once the cyclone had blown over the lab would be fully intact.

And all the while the wind picked up and the sea grew greyer, its angry surf pounding against Piccolo's shoreline. Thunder roared around them and lightning forked across the sky. The air was heavy with humidity and crackling with a menacing electrical tension that was as awesome as it was terrifying. Mary was promising to put on quite a show.

The clouds developed an ominous green tinge before darkening further into night. Streaks of lightning lit up the heavens while they ate their evening meal of sandwiches and tinned fruit together.

A chill ran through Isobella as the wind buffeted her body. She wished she could put it down to the barely leashed fury of Mary. But mostly it was the thought that tonight Alex Zaphirides' sleeping place on the beach was not an option.

Tonight he would be in her room. Tonight he would be on top.

CHAPTER SEVEN

No SOONER had they finished eating their meals than the heavens finally opened, unleashing an assault of stinging torrential rain. They couldn't have stayed out much longer anyway—the wind really was becoming too strong for human habitation. Isobella could feel the unbridled strength of it, its angry fingers pushing against her body as they raced to get inside. It was hard to imagine that the worst of it was to come.

It was only eight o'clock, and a long, fraught night stretched before them.

'Looks like it's early to bed for all of us,' Theresa said as they reached the anteroom. She shook the water droplets out of her hair. Sam's sleeping form was completely unfazed by the fury of mother nature railing around them, his head lolling with the movements.

'Where's Mike?' Alex asked.

'He's doing a last-minute check of the lab,' Theresa replied.

Everyone trooped to their rooms, carrying kerosene lanterns. They each had a supply of kerosene and matches in their bunkrooms.

'Do you want the shower first?' Alex asked.

Isobella shook her head. 'I had one before tea.'

They reached their door. 'I'll wait here until you've changed,' Alex murmured. He hoped it sounded casual, and that the slight tremor in his voice could be put down to his damaged vocal cords instead of images of Isobella stripping down to her leopard print underwear.

Isobella nodded, not looking at him, her hand stilling on the doorknob. A squall of emotions rivaling the force of Mary lashed her insides.

Alex saw her hesitation. 'I can sleep in the lab,' he offered. How was he going to sleep anyway, with her and her damn lingerie only metres away? Even way down on the beach sleep had proved elusive the last two nights.

She shivered, the erotic scrape of his voice teasing her bowstring-taut nerves back into languid relaxation. She opened the door to their room and the wild wind howling around the building rattled the taped window with ferocious intent, snapping her nerves tight again.

She'd be lying if she didn't admit that being on a small tropical island about to be sideswiped by a mighty cyclone didn't freak her out a little. Having never lived in the tropics, she'd hadn't fully appreciated the sheer raw power of weather. Her nights were too often filled with ICU flashbacks as it was. She really didn't want to ride out a cyclone alone.

'No. Mike wants us to all stay together.' She didn't look back as she entered the room and closed the door behind her.

She took the light with her, and Alex was left in the pitch-black of the narrow hallway. He leaned back into the wall, trying not to think about the fact that she was getting out of her voluminous sarong and shapeless shirt and into God knew what. The last couple of days it had been tense between them, since their argument. But it hadn't stopped him wanting to strip away her clothes and look at the real her. And not just the physical, but at whatever it was that lay behind the mask she showed to the world.

And quite why he wanted to know her like that he wasn't about to even analyse. All he knew for sure was that Isobella Nolan had intrigued him from the beginning, and her elusiveness only made him want to know more. He couldn't remember if any woman had ever got to him this much. Not even Sonya. But then no one had ever really played so hard to get.

'You can come in now.'

Alex heard her muffled words and took a few seconds to brace himself against the solidness of the wall behind him before he faced her. He was more than aware it might be the only stable part of his night. A cyclone raged outside, and a battle to rival it was raging inside him.

The glow from the lamp greeted him as he opened the door. He deliberately paid no attention to Isobella, although he could see she was lying on her bed with her knees drawn up and some papers balanced against them. He foraged through his bag on the top bunk, gathering a change of clothes quickly.

Isobella was excruciatingly aware of the solid warmth of Alex's body within touching distance. She turned her head, even though she'd been determined not to. His body from armpits down was right there. She could look her fill and he'd never know. His flat abs beneath his snug-fitting

T-shirt. His narrow hips and the enticing bulge beneath his boardies. Her fingers tingled. What would he do if she reached out and touched him?

'I'll just hit the shower,' Alex said, stepping back so he could peer down at her.

Isobella snapped her eyes forward, shocked at her wayward thoughts. Was the disrupted weather pattern altering her personality? Like a full moon? Short circuiting her tightly controlled sensibilities? 'Okay,' she said, with as much un-interest as she could muster.

Alex had almost tripped at the look that had been on Isobella's face before she had turned away. Even through her giant glasses he had seen the treacle consistency of her molasses gaze. He reached the bathroom, his heart thundering as he climbed in the shower and turned it on cold.

Isobella tapped her foot against her mattress, waiting for Alex to return. Wanting it and not wanting it at the same time. She took off her glasses and rubbed her eyes. The research figures in front of her blurred. She sighed and placed them back on her nose, forcing herself to concentrate on the report about the effects of global warming on the Crown Of Thorns starfish population of the Great Barrier Reef, which Theresa had given her to read.

The room was warm, and she shifted restlessly beneath the sheet. Without the benefit of being able to open the window and let in the cool sea breeze the humidity made lying under covers uninviting. But damned if she was going to kick them off. This was as exposed to Alex as she was ever going to be, no matter how much her raging libido urged otherwise. Maybe when he'd settled for the night she could kick her leg out.

He entered the room again and she steadfastly ignored him. His satiny boxers drew level with her line of peripheral vision, his powerful quads beautifully delineated and sprinkled with dark hair an arm's length away, and she gripped the edges of the report to stop herself from looking or touching. She breathed a sigh of relief when he finally hauled himself up onto his bunk.

The metal-framed bed squeaked and swayed a little as he moved around, getting comfortable. Her bunk moved in rhythm with his, and she shut her eyes, waiting for him to stop, trying to figure out if the movement or his proximity was causing the room to tilt. She opened them again abruptly as her mind was filled with images of being rocked by Alex in a much more intimate way.

He finally settled, and Isobella resolutely returned her attention to the paper, ploughing through it determinedly, tuned in to every fidget and page-turn from above.

After an hour of complete silence Isobella was surprised to find her eyelids growing heavy.

She would have thought she was too wired to sleep, what with gale force winds howling around the island and rattling the window and Alex's presence looming large above her, causing its own barometric upset. But the glow from the lamp pushed soft light into all the corners of the room, creating a cosy haven from the inclement elements seething outside.

She felt peculiarly safe, cocooned in a warm bubble, and although Alex's proximity was unsettling it was also perversely comforting. Reading like this was…companionable. Intimate. As if they'd been lovers for a long time and didn't need to fill the silence with words. She smiled to herself as the pages slipped from her fingers and her day of hard graft finally caught up with her.

At eleven o'clock Alex could stand the pretence of reading no longer. He hadn't heard any movements from below him for a while, so he assumed

Isobella was sleeping. He looked down past the edge of his bed and immediately wished he hadn't.

She'd turned on her side, facing the wall, and had half kicked off her sheet. Her top leg angled out of the covers in something resembling the recovery position, and a cheeky portion of her left buttock was on display. Alex lay back against his pillow and groaned. She was wearing the leopard print.

He shut his eyes hard, curling his fists into his palms, resisting the urge to take another peek. He half sat and pulled his T-shirt off, hurling it to the end of the bed. The room had been warm, but now it was positively stifling.

He battled with his will for a while longer, admitting finally that he just wasn't strong enough. He looked again. One long, bare leg greeted him, the gentle light gilding her skin with a creamy finish. The black lace of her knickers had ridden up, barely covering her exposed cheek, revealing the rounded delight of her delicate rump in all its glory.

Her top had ridden up slightly, to reveal the small of her back. He could see a glimpse of bony spine, the dip of her waist, the curve of her hip. A bare arm and shoulder were just as fascinating, her black bra strap clearly visible beneath the shoestring straps of the singlet top.

She murmured in her sleep and shifted slightly, and Alex pulled his head back sharply, his heart racing.

What the hell was he doing? She was a colleague. He was her boss, damn it!

He raised himself up on his elbow and twisted to turn off the kerosene lamp on the shelf. The room was instantly plunged into inky blackness, and he lay wide awake, praying for sleep he knew was never going to come.

Isobella was dreaming. The same dream. It was dark. The same cloying darkness that waited for her too frequently when she shut her eyes. The darkness that even when she woke, she couldn't escape. She couldn't move, couldn't open her eyes to ward off the blackness before it dragged her under again. She railed against it, moaning her frustration, her fear.

And the noises were there too. The same noises, echoing around her head. Surreal, disjointed, coming from far away, but trapped in her head for her to relive over and over. Wind and rushing and sucking and spitting and a low-level white noise that never, *never* went away. She shook her head, desperately trying to wake, to rid her mind of the noises, a sob escaping from her throat.

And the powerlessness came again. Trapped in the strange no-man's land between slumber and consciousness she felt it at its most potent. She knew her body wasn't hers any more, that other people controlled it—the people who were responsible for the noises. It was frustrating, and she whimpered, trying to get them to stop.

Talking around her as if she was dead, as if she didn't matter. Snippets of conversation, incoherent words, talking about her. Big words, grave tones. And she couldn't wake herself up to tell them she was fine. Their talk scared her, and she moaned against the heavy weight of fear settling against her chest, paralysing her lungs. She couldn't breathe.

A loud thud outside the window pierced the grip of her dream and she was startled into full consciousness, vaulting up on to her elbows. A mix between a cry and a gasp for breath left her throat before she could call it back.

Alex's eyes, not long closed, flew open. 'Isobella?'

Isobella stared into the oppressive blackness,

completely disorientated. Where was she? She could see nothing. Oh, God, was she still trapped in her dream? Was she still in hospital?

'Isobella?'

The scratchy voice came again. Alex? What was he doing here, in her dream? Her night-mare? 'A...Alex?'

He sat up, alarmed at the tremble in her voice. She sounded terrified. 'Are you okay?'

Isobella grappled for orientation. She was on Piccolo. There was a cyclone. The noises hadn't been in her head, they'd been outside. The howling of the wind, the violent smashing of the waves and the greedy slurping as they clawed at the beach before being dragged back into the ocean. There were no ventilators, no suckers, no nurses or doctors.

So why was it so dark? She lifted up her hand, waiting for her eyes to adjust so she could see it. But it was no use. Why couldn't she see it? 'It's d...dark.'

Alex still heard the tremble. 'Yes. Complete cloud cover. Long way from the bright lights. Are you...are you okay?'

No, she wasn't. The night and the noises outside were freaking her out. She took some ragged breaths to stem the spiralling anxiety that his calm explanations had not placated. 'B…bad dream. Not really.'

'Would you like some light? I can get the lamp going. There's torches here somewhere too,' he said, feeling his way down from the bunk and groping around the shelves. His hand briefly came into contact with a torch before it rolled away and then dropped to the floor, narrowly missing his foot.

The creaking of the metal frame made her jump, and the unexpected noise of the torch smashing on the ground startled her so much she cried out as adrenalin surged through her system.

'Hey,' he said softly, turning towards the direction of the bed, really concerned now about the state of her mind. He could hear her strained breathing above the wind and the rain and the surf. 'I'm sorry—I didn't mean to startle you.'

'Don't w…worry about i…it,' she stuttered, trying to bring her suddenly chattering teeth under control.

Alex sank to his knees and groped for the edge of her bunk, not caring how appropriate his behaviour was. Isobella was obviously freaked out. 'Hang on a sec,' he assured her, 'I'll get us some light.'

'No!' Her hands shook as she groped blindly through the thick cloak of night. He was close, as usual she could feel his presence, and his gravelly voice was giving her something to anchor herself to. She didn't want him to leave her side. Her fear had gone far beyond her need for light.

What she needed most now was touch. Human comfort. How many times in the ICU had she been spiralling into panic in the darkness, awake beneath all the drugs, and a soothing stroke to her forehead or a reassuring squeeze to her hand had brought her back from the brink?

Alex stopped. A hand touched his face, then his shoulder, going from tentative to grasping as she squeezed hard. He could feel her trembling, and he felt an overwhelming urge to pull her close. 'Isobella?'

She almost whimpered as she found solid muscle and clung to it. He was just there. The knowledge beat the demons back a little. 'D…don't leave.'

'I'm not going anywhere,' he assured her, gently placing a hand over hers. Her biting grip on his shoulder eased a little.

A streak of lightning lit up the sky and Alex

got a brief look at Isobella's wild-eyed face before a thunder clap shook the quarters to their very foundation. He felt the jolt of panic rip through her, felt her muscles leap as she lurched towards him.

Alex's heart thudded in his chest almost as loud as Isobella's terrified breathing against his neck. 'Hey, hey. Shh,' he crooned.

He sat with her awkwardly for a few moments, kneeling by the bed, sitting back on his heels. She was half out of bed; he was trying to support her while the rough seagrass matting bit into his knees. He shifted, trying to relieve the pressure on his knees, and her arms around his neck tightened. *This was ridiculous.*

'Move over,' he whispered, and he moved to join her.

Isobella was beyond thinking rationally about what was appropriate and professional. Or even that she'd spent the last sixteen years shying away from just this kind of situation. Right now, in her freaked-out state, she needed to feel the anchoring comfort of another human being's arms, and she couldn't think of a better solution than being totally wrapped up in him. And knowing it was pitch-black, that he couldn't see her flawed body, gave her a freedom that she hadn't known in years.

She shuffled over, closer to the wall, and felt the bed give as Alex's weight depressed the mattress.

'This is kind of squishy,' Alex muttered, trying to keep his mind off her leopard print underwear.

'I'm sorry,' she whispered.

Alex shrugged. 'I've had worse.'

Despite the cramped conditions Isobella almost cried as relief swamped her body. His presence was warm and solid beside her, and she eagerly pressed her body into the side of his. The fact that he was shirtless was secondary. He lifted his arm and she nestled her head on his chest, his hand resting protectively around her shoulders.

She could hear the bang of his heart beneath her ear and it was wonderfully grounding. The wild weather receded. The unholy racket made by the howling wind, the pouring rain and the pounding surf all faded away. Just the steady drum of Alex's heartbeat filled her head.

'Talk to me,' she whispered.

Alex shut his eyes. He could hear the tremor in her voice and feel the frantic flutter of her heartbeat against his side like a frightened bird. But with her body pressed against him it was hard to keep her anxiety in focus. He seriously doubted whether he was capable of anything as complex as speech. Breathing at the moment seemed to be a challenge. 'Do you want to…do you want to talk about the dream?'

'No!' Adrenalin still buzzed through her system. She just wanted to cling to him and relegate the nightmare to the dark reaches of her brain.

'Okay, okay,' he soothed, patting her shoulder, feeling the fine trembling of her muscles there. 'So what *do* you want to talk about?'

'Anything. Anything but that. Say something in Greek.'

He almost groaned. How many times had he heard that request when sharing a bed with a woman? Somehow he didn't think Isobella had that kind of talk in mind. Alex prayed for restraint. '*The Iliad*, perhaps?'

Isobella's laugh sounded strained even to her own ears. 'Maybe not. A fairy tale or a nursery rhyme? Wasn't Aesop Greek? Maybe a fable?'

Alex sighed and launched into *The Wolf in Sheep's Clothing*, not stopping to question the irony of his choice. Here he was, lying next to her, her half-naked body superglued to his side, pretending to be some fine upstanding gentleman rescuing a damsel in distress. When the reality was he wanted nothing more than to strip away her clothes and chase the cyclone into the night with a little earth-moving of his own.

She was quiet when he'd finished the story and he wondered if she had fallen asleep. He hadn't consciously realised but he'd been trailing his fingers up and down her arm as he'd spoken, and they stilled now. He strained to hear her breath, gratified to find that it seemed more modulated now.

'Tell me about hospital.'

Alex's first instinct was to reject her request out of hand. He didn't talk about that time. It was private. He hadn't told anybody about the dark times, when he'd despaired for his life. Not a soul. He'd never got close enough to another human being to feel comfortable enough about unloading.

But if ever there was a time and a place to do so, now felt pretty right. Her hair was tickling his chin, and the realisation that they were both in unfamiliar territory, both just trying to get through the night, helped. He knew enough about Isobella to know that whatever demons were in her head had to be bad for her to be plastered against him. So maybe she knew something about demons.

And he needed to keep his mind off her leopard print underwear somehow.

'It was probably one of the most humbling experiences of my life.'

Isobella had closed her eyes, having given up on him answering. She opened them, staring into the inky darkness. 'How so?' she murmured.

'Being the one lying in a bed taught me a lot about medicine that I never would have learned otherwise.'

'Like what?'

Her breath was warm against his chest. 'Patience, humility, that doctors don't know everything.'

She let that sink in. Surgeons weren't known for their humility. 'Did you have chemo?'

Alex nodded. 'I had some node involvement. I had chemo and radium.'

His husky words softened the ugliness of their meaning, but Isobella felt compelled to comfort him anyway. She draped her arm across his chest, her hand resting on the warm round prominence of his opposite shoulder. 'Sounds bad.'

Alex lay very still as her fingers absently stroked his skin. 'It was.'

She was quiet for a few moments, absorbing his brief but angst-loaded words. She listened to the suck of the waves on the beach that had so freaked her out in the darkness not that long ago. 'So what else did you learn?'

Alex thought for a moment. 'I learnt who my friends were.'

Isobella felt him tense beneath her touch even before the bitterness in his tone affected her. 'Sonya?'

His lips twisted as Sonya's betrayal revisited him. 'She barely waited until I'd been shifted from Intensive Care before she gave me back my ring. Told me she hadn't signed up for an invalid.'

Isobella gave a horrified gasp. 'Ouch.'

Alex gave a half-laugh. 'Indeed. Sonya wanted the glamour of being Dr and Mrs—the prestige of being married to a hotshot surgeon. She hadn't counted on the worse part of *for better or worse* rearing its ugly head quite so soon.'

Isobella cringed. 'I'm sorry.'

He remembered how she'd apologised over

the same thing at the hotel. 'Don't be.' He was surprised how little it hurt now, when it had gutted him so badly a decade ago. 'It made me a better person. The cancer. Sonya. It taught me two important lessons.'

'Oh?'

'Life's short. And guard your heart closely.'

Her chest ached for him. 'We're not all like that, you know.' She would *never* have squandered his love. Left him when he needed her most. 'Not all women leave.'

Funnily enough, lying here next to her like this, he could almost believe it. There'd been an honesty between them tonight that had never existed between him and Sonya. Maybe she was right? Still, the first cut was always the deepest.

'I'd prefer not to put it to the test again. I think I'll stick with my game plan.'

'Ah. That would be the old catch-kiss-and-throw-back game plan?'

Alex chuckled at the derision in her voice. 'That would be it.'

Isobella yawned. The last thing she wanted right now was to get into a discussion about the idiocy of his theory, when her avoidance of fishing altogether wasn't any more healthy.

'I wonder what the time is?' she murmured.

Alex lifted his arm and pushed a button on the side of his watch. 'Nearly one a.m.'

They were silent for a few minutes, contemplating the long night still ahead of them. 'Thank you, Alex,' she whispered.

Alex nodded. 'Are you sure you don't want to talk about the dream?'

Isobella shook her head. 'Thanks, but no.' What good would it do? 'I think I'm just going to go to sleep.'

Alex listened as her breathing evened out and her head grew heavy against his chest. He envied her that as he lay awake, staring into the impossible blackness and listening to the storm rage outside whilst simultaneously ignoring the one raging inside him.

Alex's eyelids snapped open an hour later. The noise from the Cyclone was disorientating, and it took a second or two to realise what exactly had woken him. Isobella's hand had crept perilously close to a part of his anatomy that was now more than aware of her nearness. He was painfully hard. He swallowed, shutting his eyes and reaching for a modicum of sanity.

She muttered something in her sleep and shifted, her knuckles grazing the length of him. He opened his eyes again, and bit his lip to stifle a groan. He tried hard not to think about her grasping his erection, running her hand up and down the length of it, testing its girth, relishing in its contours.

Enough! He might be practising his gentlemanly ways, but there were limits!

He gingerly picked up her lifeless, uninterested hand and removed it from the proximity of his very interested appendage. She muttered something and then shifted, rolling on her side, her back to him. Alex was so grateful that all her interesting bits were now not squashed into him that he too rolled on his side, his back to her back.

At least it would make it easier to sleep.

CHAPTER EIGHT

ANOTHER hour passed, and Isobella woke to utter blackness. She was conscious that they'd both moved during their sleep. She was on her side, Alex's arm heavy around her waist, his frame curled around hers. The noises from outside still raged. The wind whipped around the building like a hundred angry ghosts, and the sea pounded its fury against the shore.

But she was safe and warm in Alex's embrace. The nightmare of earlier had completely receded, and she snuggled back against him. She became aware of the sudden tightening of his arm at the same time she became aware of the hard rod pressed into the cleft of her bottom.

She stilled, even as her heart pounded clear out of her chest. The evidence of his arousal was as fascinating as it was terrifying. The lab geek in her wanted to leap out of bed and cross herself, but the woman, the lacy lingerie woman, who despite her best efforts still thrived beneath the white-coated exterior, wanted to move again, stretch against him, reach for him.

Was he even awake? Men got erections in their sleep without their knowledge all the time. Everyone knew that—it was just a fact of life. It had nothing to do with her as a woman and everything to do with a man's biology and diurnal rhythms. He'd probably have an erection at this hour of the morning regardless of whether she was there or not.

Still, she'd be lying if she didn't admit that part of her, the vain ex-model part, wanted it to be because of her. And before she could stop herself she wiggled against him. Alex's erection surged against her, and she could have sworn she heard him groan.

'Alex?'

'Quit moving.' Alex was awake again. Very awake. *God, this night was going on for ever.*

The low growl slithered down her spine. His lips were just beside her ear. She turned her head to apologise, but even that slight twist bought their pelvises together again, causing a delightful friction.

'Damn it, Isobella, don't do that.'

He was just flesh and blood. Didn't she realise what kind of fire she was playing with? Her body was loose and relaxed for a change, and the way the cheeks of her bottom cradled him was as sinful as the waft of her perfume. Her head was tucked firmly beneath his chin, and the urge to bury his face in her neck, to kiss her there, was overwhelming. He removed his arm and rolled on to his back, putting temptation out of reach. Sort of.

Isobella noted the strain in his voice even as she lamented the loss of contact. He sounded annoyed. And of course he had a right to be. This must be his worst nightmare. Having to babysit an employee who had become a screaming nutter on him, and then being put in a position where his normal bodily functions embarrassed him.

She silently cringed. She had to make this better. They had to work together, for crying out loud. She opened her eyes, staring into the dark abyss, and rolled over towards him, propping herself up on her elbow.

'I'm sorry, Alex. This isn't your fault. I understand. You don't have to worry. I know that men have…urges that come upon them with no real control a lot of the time. It's okay, we both have medical backgrounds and we're both adults. I know you're…you're…just experiencing normal night-time activity. You're a healthy male with…normal male appetites, and this…this…problem has nothing to do with me personally but…'

Alex listened to her stuttering and stammering through her speech, making as much of a wreck of it as Cyclone Mary was to Piccolo. What the hell was she going on about? 'Isobella, what are you talking about?'

'I'm just saying…I don't want you to feel awkward about this. I'm not going to get any…fancy ideas about you…you…desiring me…I know this is just a normal male response…a physiological occurrence…'

Isobella was pleased for the darkness for the first time tonight as her cheeks heated up. She was making a total hash of it.

Alex frowned. *What the—?* Physiological occurrence? Normal night-time activity? Did she seriously think his hard on was anything other than pure male lust for the woman in his bed, plastered to his side? The woman who'd been driving him crazy for the last week? She'd been hiding behind those clothes for too long.

'Isobella,' he said patiently, barely making out her face in the inky night. 'I can assure you this has nothing to do with male rhythms.'

Isobella wasn't sure if it was the erotic scrape of his words on her skin, the latent electricity from the storm outside or what he'd said, but suddenly there was a hum in her blood, prickling at her skin.

'Of course it is,' she babbled nervously. Because what if it wasn't? She didn't want to think about what if it wasn't…

She'd had a crush on this man for ever. The last man who'd desired her had run away at a very crucial moment, and even though she was safe from that humiliation in the blackened room the mere thought that Alex might desire her back was beyond her conception.

'No. It's not.'

Isobella swallowed at the gravelly denial, trying to talk and breathe and think double-time to convince him he was only experiencing a natural phenomena. 'I can see why you might be confused. I mean, I read this study once—'

'Isobella.'

'No, no,' she insisted. 'It was really very inter-esting. They were looking at male arousal patterns, and did these studies on mon-keys, and—'

Alex raised his head in the general direction of her voice, found her lips and kissed her. Hard.

Isobella was too stunned to pull away. Too stunned to even join in. Her brain activity froze as a surge of undiluted desire turned every-thing to sludge.

No, no, no. Pull back, pull back, pull back.

With superhuman effort Isobella broke away. She was breathing hard, still fighting through the fog in her brain. She could hear Alex's breath-ing too. His face was still close, she could feel his warm breath on her cheek.

'Look, Alex, r…really this is normal male be-haviour.' Isobella finally broke the silence, her voice almost as husky as his. 'You don't have to pretend it's anything else. That study said—'

He kissed her again. Quick and hard. 'Shut up, Isobella.' He ran his thumb over the swollen contours of her mouth and was gratified to hear a faint whimper somewhere in the back of her throat. 'This isn't about male arousal patterns or physiology or monkeys. This is about me wanting you.' He kissed her again briefly, for good measure, pleased to feel the almost slavish way she responded. 'And you wanting me.'

His voice coming out at her from the inky night seemed even more sinful. Like a whisper in the dark. He wanted her. And he knew she wanted him.

'So what are we going to do about it?'

His voice growled low in her ear, and her fingers curled into her palm as her lower abdominal muscles squeezed tight. She wanted to devour him on the spot. Years of celibacy and an ugly duckling complex had made her ripe for this moment. Alex Zaphirides wanted her. Alex Zaphirides, who could have anyone. It just didn't make sense.

'Are you sure this isn't an any port in a storm thing?'

Alex sighed. 'Isobella, I've been wanting to get your god-awful clothes off all week.'

Isobella supposed she should take offence at his dig over her clothes, but the revelation that he'd wanted her all week stirred her long-suppressed hormones and completely blunted her cognitive powers.

'But why?' Once upon a time she wouldn't have had to ask that question, but it had been a long time since a man had noticed her.

He heard the genuine bewilderment in her voice. She sounded small and impossibly young in the big, dark night. 'Maybe because I can see beneath all that camouflage? Behind the big glasses, baggy clothes and white coat. You are a beautiful woman, Isobella Nolan.'

How many years had it been since she'd been told that? She'd heard it so often in her younger years she'd never really appreciated it. Until now. And Alex Zaphirides thought she was beautiful.

Her hand was on his bare chest, resting near his shoulder, and he was warm and solid. And he wanted her. He thought she was beautiful. Was he spinning her some pretty lies? No. She believed him. She'd heard enough false platitudes during her modelling years to know sincerity when she heard it.

'Isobella?'

She heard the question in his raspy voice. The ball was in her court. The sensible thing, of course, would be to get out of bed right now and put as much distance between them as possible. He was her boss, and it was entirely inappropriate. But how often had she dreamed about this? How often had she denied herself the normal urges of a healthy young woman?

It could only be tonight. She knew that. Alex had made himself more than clear on his attitude to relationships, and she wasn't stupid enough to think that she would be any more than one of Alex's catch-kiss-and-throw-back girls. And that was fine. In fact it might be just what the doctor had ordered. Get this unhealthy crush out of her system once and for all. And then get back to what was really important—her work.

And what better place then here in the pitch-black? In this haven safe from the raging cyclone and her past? Here she could be an equal. Not poor, scarred Isobella, to pity or recoil from, but a woman indulging her sexual side free from all her usual bodily hang-ups. In the darkness she could be Izzy again.

Emboldened by the impenetrable night and by years of suppressing her feminine side, she trailed her hand down his chest.

Alex felt each and every muscle ripple beneath her hand in turn as it passed over them. 'Isobella.'

The gravel in his voice was like the rub of sandpaper against her belly, her nipples, her inner thigh. She inched lower.

Alex swallowed as her finger prodded at the waistband to his boxers. 'Isobella…'

She heard the strained warning and it somehow made her bolder. She pushed into his boxers and her fingers sought a way into his underwear.

Alex swallowed as the tips of her fingers grazed his swollen head. 'Isobella.'

This time it was a groan. A groan so ragged it was a physical entity stroking, deep inside her. She finally reached her destination, her hand nudging the solid length of him and then enclosing him, her palm filling with his girth.

She sighed and squeezed. He felt like velvet over steel and her hand revelled in the sensation. The moan rumbling from his mouth empowered her further. She moved her closed hand down the length of him. Then back up again. Then down again.

'Isobella!' Alex was almost delirious from her touch. It was torture. 'You'd better be prepared to follow through if you keep doing—'

It was her turn to interrupt him, cutting him off with her mouth, softly at first, tentatively, then with growing confidence as his mouth joined in, his head lifting off the bed to devour her more thoroughly. She broke away as dizziness spun stars in front of her. 'How was that for follow-through?' she teased.

Alex grinned into the darkness. The taste of her on his lips was making him greedy for more as he speared his fingers into her hair.

He raised his mouth again to plunder her lips, driven by her hand squeezing, stroking, teasing his hardness. Their passion ignited, their kisses elevating to even more feverish planes. Alex could bear the torture of her hand no longer, and flipped her on to her back in the narrow bed, kicking out of his clothes.

'Oh.' Isobella clutched at his shoulders as he settled his naked pelvis against the cradle of hers, his erection pushing against her. His mouth rejoined hers and she dug her fingers into his bare back as his mouth wreaked havoc on her lips, her face, her neck.

The ridge of his hardness taunted her. She squirmed, rubbing herself against him, trying to get closer, trying to ease the ache, the burning between her legs that only he could extinguish.

Alex pushed his hand beneath her shirt, inching it up out of the way as his fingers felt the ridges between each rib. He hit soft satin. 'I wish I could see you,' he groaned against her mouth as he kissed down her neck. He wanted to see what her breasts looked like encased in black satin and leopard print, and then he wanted to watch as they fell free into his eager hands, his eager mouth.

Isobella moaned out loud as he pushed the bra cups up out of the way in the general direction of her shirt. His mouth closed over a nipple and she was exceedingly grateful for the eerie blackness. It was the only way this would be possible for her. This way she got to be beautiful in his eyes—not scarred or a victim or a freak. This way she got to be the woman she'd always been underneath. The one who adored fine silks and lace against her skin. Passionate. Desirable. Beautiful.

He moved lower, dropping kisses down the centre of her stomach, his hands still stroking the fullness of her breasts. She felt the heat between her legs crank up even further in anticipation. Her hands raked through his hair, feeling the sensuous glide of his locks against the sensitive pads of her fingers.

He traversed her belly, pressing searing kisses there, and she tensed despite the impossible blackness around her. The scars weren't raised, and she knew there was no way he could make them out in this light, but years of conditioning had taken their toll.

'You're beautiful,' he murmured against her belly, turning his head to kiss the slope of her hip. He'd known she'd be like this under all those layers—smooth and supple and soft. His body warred with the desire to be inside her. But he wanted to taste every inch of her. He wanted to *see* every inch of her, and cursed the darkness.

His mouth reached the bow on her knickers and he laved it with his tongue, torn between ripping it off and undoing it with his teeth. Her scent was driving him wild, and her moans were making him crazy. He hooked his finger under the waistband of her knickers and peeled them off.

'Alex!' Isobella cried out as her underwear fell away. She wanted to feel him in her. She needed it. Needed it more than she needed anything. Right now if someone offered her the secret formula she's been searching for the last two years she'd dismiss it out of hand. Only Alex mattered.

Alex kissed his way back up, stopping to lave her breasts with more attention, pulling her nipples into his eager mouth, wishing he could gaze upon their splendour. Would her nipples be rosy or dusky? And how would they look after he'd worshipped them, all swollen and moist?

She whimpered, and he raised his head to kiss her mouth, swallowing another noise of desperation coming from the back of her throat. He knew how she felt. He was lost in a swirling vortex of pleasure mimicking the cyclone outside, helpless against its pull, at the mercy of its whims.

They were both too needy. It would be too quick. But he didn't know how to slow it down. His sex nudged hers, and he shuddered as slickness and heat enveloped the head of his throbbing shaft.

Isobella tensed. This was it. The moment she'd been waiting for. She felt a moment's hesitation. It had been so long. What if she wasn't... adequate?

Alex's mouth broke from hers. Pressed against her this intimately, he had sensed her slight recoil. 'Isobella? What is it?'

Cold feet? Second thoughts? Oh, God! He leant his forehead against hers, struggling to control his breath. He didn't know how to put this tiger back in its cage.

Isobella too gulped for air, amazed at his ability to interpret even her slight hesitation. She thought about saying nothing, but this close—their foreheads touching, their noses touching, their lips a whisker apart—she couldn't do it. If ever there was a moment for honesty this was it.

'It's…it's been a long time…for me.'

Alex hissed out a breath. Was that all? He remembered her celibacy comment. He kissed her. 'How long?'

Isobella shied from the truth. She and Paolo had been lovers for six months before the day of her accident. He had been her first and her last. Anthony had fled in horror before they'd ever consummated their relationship. Would Alex think that terribly gauche of her? One lover sixteen years ago?

'Years,' she finally admitted, shying from putting an actual figure on it.

Alex barely heard her whispered response above the noise of the storm. 'Oh, Isobella,' he murmured, running his nose across her cheeks and over her eyelids. He kissed her forehead, feeling greatly honoured to be the man to reintroduce her to the pleasures of the flesh. 'We'll take it slow. I promise. Wrap your legs around me.'

His gravelly request twisted her pelvic floor muscles, and as he kissed her again she did as he asked. His pelvis settling into hers as if he'd been made to do so.

'Easy, now,' he whispered, his mouth at her ear as he positioned himself and slowly sank into her tight, moist heat. Her nails clawed at his back, and it shot a streak of molten desire straight to his groin.

Isobella groaned as he filled her, stretched her, completed her. He whispered something she didn't understand in her ear—was it in his mother tongue? She swallowed as the gravel in his voice enhanced his accent, grazing her body from the tip of her toes to the top of her head.

He felt good. So good inside her. How had she denied herself this for so long? Or maybe she'd just been holding out for the right man? And as Alex moved inside her, with slow, gentle pushes that were tender and heartbreaking, with restraint trembling through his shoulders, she realised that she'd been waiting for him.

His voice growled low and husky in her ear, murmuring words she didn't understand. His voice was even more erotic, more sinful in the pitch-black, whispering who knew what. Were they endearments? Or something more risqué? He gave her lobe a gentle bite and she cried out, digging her nails into his naked back, her pelvic muscles contracting around him.

Alex felt her pulse against him and buried his face into the side of her neck. He couldn't remember sex ever being this good. This…all-consuming. Usually it was just his body that was engaged. It knew the moves and performed them on auto-pilot.

But this was different. He wasn't used to having the woman in his head. Her generosity touching his heart. Maybe it was because he'd confessed everything to her, told her things he'd never told anyone else before. Maybe he actually felt something for her that was deeper for a change. Deeper than sex.

'Alex.'

He heard her whimper and felt her tighten around him, knew she was close to the edge. He slowed further, drawing it out, making it unbearably erotic, impossibly sweet.

'Alex!'

He smiled at her tortured exclamation. Winced at the nails digging into his back. Gripped the mattress in an effort to control his strokes. 'Hush,' he murmured.

'I can't,' she cried. 'I can't. I think I'm… Oh, God! Oh, Alex!'

He felt the second she snapped, her breath rushing out in a gasp, her body bucking against his, clamping down on his length. She cried out his name and he held her earthbound as pleasure rained down around her almost as violently as the torrential downpour outside.

Her muscles stroked him, pulled him deep inside her, sucked him in further, closer. His own desire was spinning out of control, rushing up to meet hers. He wanted to hold out, to give her centre stage, but her abandon was his complete undoing and he followed her into it.

His orgasm hit him square in the solar plexus, making it impossible to breathe, impossible to do anything other than mindlessly pound into her like the waves beating against the shore. Every muscle tautened unbearably. His chest ached, his heart thundered, racing against the storm, trying to outlast it and failing miserably.

'Alex,' Isobella gasped, her breathing still ragged as the last of her climax undulated through her internal muscles. She felt another little shock wave and revelled in the feel of Alex still filling her.

'Thank you,' she whispered, staring into the black night in front of her, the contours of his face barely visible.

'No,' he murmured, kissing her nose, her cheek, her eyelids. 'Thank *you.*' Her response had been gratifying on a whole other level. He hadn't known sex could be so utterly fulfilling.

Isobella smiled, her eyelids fluttering closed as a languid lassitude infused her bones, making them heavy. Somewhere in her consciousness she could hear the storm still raging. 'Stay with me,' she whispered.

Alex heard the drowsiness in her voice and felt a similar lethargy infect him. He moved off her and turned as she turned, pulling her close. They spooned, his arm around her, his fingers firmly interlocked with hers. And when he shut his eyes he let memories of their lovemaking carry him into slumber.

Isobella woke to a grey light throwing an eerie gloom into the room. She could hear the wind and the pound of the surf, although it seemed to have settled considerably. She wondered what the time was and swallowed against a dry throat.

She was alone in the bed. Alone with her thoughts. Her demons. She hadn't moved since she'd fallen asleep with Alex wrapped around her. Her bra was still skewed, although her shirt had ridden down to cover her breasts. Her knickers were God knew where, and she was pleased to find a sheet covering her. They hadn't gone to sleep covered, so Alex must have pulled it up.

She looked down at the scarring on her abdomen and thanked God that she'd still been facing away from Alex when he left. He had learned a lot about her last night, wrapped in their dark cocoon, and it hadn't seemed real. But in the cold light of day some things were still too private. Some things were still out of bounds. If they'd been entering into a relationship—maybe? But a roll in the hay on a stormy night?

She wondered where Alex was. No doubt somewhere completely freaked out about them giving in to temptation last night. How would he be when she saw him again? Would he avoid eye contact, or maybe just avoid her, period?

He had nothing to fear from her. She knew the score. Yes, something special had happened between them last night—at least it had for her. Something she was not going to analyse for a long time. But he was a man. A catch-kiss-and-throw-back man at that. And he was her boss, and they had to work together. They'd crossed a lot of lines. It was time she assured him that she knew where the line was and how to get back behind it.

She showered quickly, donning her standard lab geek camouflage. She hoped her reversion back to her usual dress would convince him of her serious intent to put what had happened last night behind them. Actions spoke louder than words, didn't they?

Although that was a kind of a dangerous notion to explore at the moment. What had her actions told him last night? What had his actions told her? That it was more than illicit sex between colleagues or a way to pass a stormy night? He had touched her reverently, been gentle and restrained. Understanding. His actions hadn't said catch-kiss-and-throw-back. What they'd actually said she wasn't sure, but they hadn't been those of a man interested only in seminar sex.

She exited the building to find everyone up and about. The wind blew against her body and she braced herself. But whilst it was strong it was obviously not gale force, and though the sea was still choppy and the waves against the shore were sizeable, Cyclone Mary had moved on. The rain had also stopped. For now.

She performed a quick visual survey of the

nearby buildings, pleased to see they appeared to have escaped Mary's wrath unscathed. There was a lot of felled foliage—branches and general green debris—but no major damage was evident.

She swivelled her head towards the beach and the pounding surf. A line of thick seaweed marked the shore, obviously spewed forth from the churning seas along with some driftwood. The tide was going out. The deeper water looked a menacing grey.

Her gaze fell upon Alex, a little further down the beach, staring out over the waves, his dark hair blowing in the wind. His fingers were buried deeply in his pockets, his shoulders were hunched. Was he wishing himself off Piccolo?

She hugged herself as she walked towards him. The air was cooler now the immediate low pressure system had moved away, and the strong wind was caressing her exposed forearms. She shivered—was it the wind, or her trepidation as Alex grew larger?

Isobella drew level with him. He didn't acknowledge her, and they both stared out to sea for a few moments. 'Hi,' she finally greeted him, raising her voice a little to be heard over the crash of the surf.

'Hi.' He didn't turn to look at her. His thoughts churned as restlessly as the ocean.

'The island appears to have escaped relatively unscathed,' she said.

'Yes. Mike and I are going to go for a reccie a little later on, but everything seems to have come through okay.'

Isobella nodded. They'd been lucky.

Alex cleared his throat. 'About last night…'

For a moment her heart stopped. It stuttered to a halt in her chest before kicking in again at a faster rate. His voice scraped deliciously along her nerves. She ignored it, placing a hand on his arm as she took a measured breath. 'It's okay. I know what you're going to say and I really don't need you to.'

'Oh?' Alex certainly hadn't expected this. Even seeing her in her don't-look-at-me clothes and glasses he felt his desire return. It was no use now—he was always going to know the secrets of the body under her white coat. Always going to want it.

'Please, Alex.' She turned to him, forcing a casual smile. He looked devastating this morning. He was wearing a white shirt unbuttoned, flapping in the breeze. She wanted him to take her again. Right here, right now. 'It was a one-off. I was scared. You were comforting me. One thing led to another.'

He frowned. 'It did.'

'I understand. What happens on Piccolo stays on Piccolo. You don't need to worry.'

'Right.'

Alex was answering automatically, unsure of his place on the page. He'd been practising his own speech since he'd risen this morning, with her round naked bottom tucked into him. How inappropriate it had been. How wrong. All the reasons why it couldn't be any more than it was. The same words he'd said to a lot of women. But then she'd joined him and memories of last night had clawed at him and the words had withered.

Isobella frowned at the uncertainty in his voice. 'Isn't that the way you like it—catch-kiss-and-throw-back?'

Usually, yes. Usually it was exactly the way he liked it. His frown deepened as the scary thought that maybe for once he wanted more entered his consciousness. No. He wouldn't give another woman power over him again. Sonya had cured him of that. 'What if you're pregnant?'

Isobella gasped. 'What?'

Alex was a little shocked himself. He hadn't been expecting that to come out of his mouth. He shrugged. 'We didn't use any protection.'

Isobella placed a hand on her stomach. They hadn't, had they? She'd been too frightened to think logically—contraception had never crossed her mind. Her womb suddenly ached at the thought of carrying Alex's child. 'I doubt that'll be an issue,' she said, her lips twisting.

Alex heard the derision in her voice. 'Oh?'

Isobella shook her head. 'Wrong time of the month,' she lied. It was easier.

Alex nodded, surprised at how disappointed he was. 'So you're okay with all this? Just act like it never happened?'

Isobella steeled herself to look at him with absolute assurance. 'Perfectly. Aren't you?'

Alex snorted. He did this habitually. He knew the rules better than anyone—he'd written them. 'Sure.'

'Good,' Isobella confirmed. 'I'll see you later, then.'

She turned away and trudged up the beach before she changed her mind, determinedly leaving behind the best time she'd ever had.

CHAPTER NINE

IT WAS two days before they could leave Piccolo.
Two days before the seas calmed and the sun
came out. Isobella watched the island grow
smaller from the back of the boat, a jewel sitting
amongst crystal waters. She hugged herself.
Whatever else happened in her life, she would
always have Piccolo.

The last two days had been…strange. Pretending nothing had occurred had certainly
sounded easy at the time, but hadn't been so easy
in practice. She'd been hyperaware of his every
move, his every rumble, his every breath. He had
been painstakingly polite, collegial, professional,
but occasionally he had looked at her, and she'd
seen desire slumbering in his gaze and heat had
scorched her insides.

The nights had been the worst. Continuing rain
had prevented his return to the beach, so having

him directly above her had been a particular brand of torment. He hadn't come to bed until long after her, but if his plan had been to sneak in after she was asleep then it had failed miserably. Sleep had proved elusive. For him, too, if the frequent creaking of the bed had been any indication.

She turned away from the island, facing the activity on the boat. Alex was talking to Mike as he drove. His profile was strong, almost regal, and she wished she could go to him, wrap her arms around his waist and have him look down at her and smile.

Theresa was squatting next to Sam, redoing the life jacket clips over his red T-shirt. The impish toddler looked set to become the next Houdini. Theresa stood ruffling her son's hair, and Isobella watched as Sam's chubby arms encircled Theresa's bare brown leg. He looked up at his mother and gave her a grin that could melt a glacier.

Her hand went to her belly as Alex's comment about her being pregnant revisited. How she'd love to look down into the face of her child and see such unconditional love beamed back at her. To feel a chubby hand on her leg, soft, downy hair brushing her thigh, her palm.

She sighed, turning away to look out to sea. Was her work ever going to be enough now?

The boat headed for Temora Island. Isobella and Alex's plane was scheduled to take off at midday, and Mike and Theresa needed to pick up supplies. Piccolo Island had survived the cyclone relatively intact, but there were a few minor repairs that needed carrying out, and Mike had radioed his requirements ahead as soon as he'd assessed the damage.

The cruiser made several stops before heading for its final destination, checking on the various submerged experiment stations dotted between the two islands. Mike and Theresa were eager to see if the equipment had held up under the onslaught of the turbulent ocean. Sam, life jacket firmly in place, had been put down in the cabin for his nap so his parents could work unhindered.

They dropped anchor at their last stop, having been delayed by some running repairs required at the previous two. Isobella watched as Alex helped Mike haul up some equipment attached to a buoy via a heavy chain. They placed the dripping tank on the deck and proceeded to check the various monitoring components were all in working order.

Isobella watched Alex. The bunch of his powerful quads as he squatted beside Theresa was truly magnificent. The play of muscles in his bronzed arms as he fiddled with a thermometer was fascinating. The rumble of his voice as he asked questions was as lulling as the warm sun beating down on her shoulders.

She looked away as memories of his naked body on hers the other night swamped her. Not that she had seen his nudity, but she remembered the feel of those muscles, the contours of his frame, and still shivered at the memory of his sexy voice whispering sinful things in his mother tongue.

She was pleased she'd worn a light cotton button-up caftan shirt. It was sleeveless and allowed for the free flow of air and she certainly needed that right now, between steamy thoughts of Alex and the hot midday sun. A sea breeze ruffled the thin white fabric and it felt good against her heated skin.

Alex's cerulean gaze had darkened as he had taken it in when he'd offered his hand to help her on board, and a blush had stolen up her cheeks. It was probably the most feminine thing she owned that she wore with any regularity. Apart from her underwear.

It was plain, if rather form-fitting, emphasising instead of hiding all those features she usually avoided exposing to the world. Her full breasts, her flat stomach, her toned arms. The yoke was lightly embroided with white stitching and decorated with crystal sequins, complementing the truly feminine cut. Tiny pearl buttons ran all the way up the middle, right up to the mandarin collar, securing it safely high on her neck.

She wasn't quite sure why she'd put it on with a sarong this morning, instead of her usual baggy attire. Or why she'd even packed it. It was certainly perfect weather for it. But then it had been all along. Maybe she wanted to leave Alex with an impression of her as a woman, the woman he had taken to dizzying heights two nights ago? Not the other woman. The lab geek. But Izzy, his responsive lover.

A flash of red in her peripheral vision distracted her, and she turned her head towards its location at the back of the boat, thankful for the reprieve. She was just in time to see Sam, *sans* life jacket, losing his balance as he leaned over the side of the boat, and falling silently into the water.

'Sam!' she yelled, panic rising in her chest, her pulse roaring through her head. She sprinted towards the back, stripping off her sarong, discarding her glasses, kicking off her flip-flops.

'Isobella?' Alex called after her.

'It's Sam,' she yelled back as she reached the side searching the water quickly, looking for any sign of the little boy, praying that he would bob to the surface.

They were in the middle of the ocean—it wasn't the crystal-clear waters of the island—and just looking was futile. She hesitated for a moment, feeling the clutch of panic as her fear of the ocean and what had happened to her the last time she'd ventured in took hold.

Part of her wanted to recoil. To find a nice safe corner of the boat and pretend nothing had happened. And for a moment she hesitated, summoning the nerve to do something she hadn't done in sixteen years. Something she'd sworn she'd never do again. But Theresa's anguished cry pierced her bubble of anxiety. She took a deep breath and jumped into the water. A child's life was at stake. There was no time for hysterics.

She could vaguely hear shouting from the boat as she ducked and dived repeatedly around the area at the back of the cruiser, her under-average vision probing the vastness of the murky depths for a small, small boy.

She could hear Theresa crying as she came up for air, and felt more desperate, more helpless. There were splashes beside her as Alex and Mike joined in the search. She dived down again, holding her breath until her chest throbbed and her eyes stung from the salt water.

She burst to the surface, taking huge gulps of air. Something brushed her leg and her pulse-rate leapt, a surge of adrenalin and panic flooding her system as she waited for the pain, for the searing heat. It took a split second for her to realise the touch was harmless, and another to duck her head under the water to check out the source, her heart hammering. Could it be?

Sam's little body hung eerily suspended in the water, just near her toe. 'Here!' she called to the others, before diving down, grabbing him around the waist and kicking hard at the water to deliver them to the surface *pronto*.

Then Alex was there, congratulating her, taking the frighteningly limp child from her, kicking powerfully to the boat, passing him up to Theresa. 'I need you,' he called over his shoulder to her as he hauled himself onto the boat.

Isobella responded instantly, as she suspected she always would to Alex, and swam to the side. He leant down and pulled her onto the boat in one sleek movement. Water sluiced off her, and their bodies brushed briefly before they turned their attention to a hysterical Theresa, who was hugging Sam tight and crying uncontrollably, shaking him and telling him to wake up.

Mike was trying to pry his son out of his wife's arms, and Isobella glanced at Alex as the high emotion of the life-and-death situation enveloped her in its dreadful grip. Theresa's anguish, her raw grief, was terrible to watch.

'Theresa!'

Alex's voice might have been rough and husky, but the command growled across the boat, cutting into her hysteria. Theresa stopped crying and looked at him.

'Let Isobella and I take care of Sam.'

He held out his arms, and Isobella breathed a sigh of relief when Theresa relinquished her frighteningly still son to Alex's care.

Alex laid him on the deck and they both knelt beside him, uncaring of their dripping state. Sam lips were blue, and already his little limbs were cold and mottled. He wasn't breathing. 'How long do you reckon he's been apnoeic for?' Alex murmured quietly.

Isobella shrugged, her brain trying to rapidly calculate while at the same time assimilate how such an active little boy could look so…lifeless. 'Two minutes tops.'

'He has a faint brachial pulse,' Alex said, louder this time, trying to give Theresa hope.

Mike was holding her tight, telling her Sam was going to be all right. That he and Isobella were going to save him. Alex prayed it wasn't too late. Signs of a pulse were encouraging.

'Keep monitoring it,' Alex instructed as he dipped his head towards Sam's colourless face, grasped his chin, pinched his little nostrils and puffed air past his cold lips.

Isobella's heart drummed madly in her chest as she watched the bob of Alex's head. Reaction to her unplanned dip in the ocean warred with the desperate battle for life happening before her eyes. Now was not the time to freak out.

Sam's pulse fluttered slow and weak against her fingers as she focused her attention on the task at hand. She pushed harder against the crook of his elbow, willing it to be stronger.

'Get some blankets,' Alex ordered in between puffs. 'Something—anything—to get him warm.'

Isobella vaguely heard Theresa leave, no doubt grateful to have something to do that was going to help. Then a few seconds later Sam's body spasmed, his shoulders jerked, and he coughed.

Alex sprang back as a fountain of sea water spewed from the little boy's mouth and ran out of his nose. They quickly rolled him on his side and he started to cry. A great big beautiful wail that Isobella would never forget as long as she lived. His lips were already pinking up.

Theresa heard it, and she flew across the deck, sobbing his name.

'Mummy,' Sam wailed, between coughing and spluttering.

'It's okay, darling. Mummy's here,' Theresa choked, cocooning her son in the large beach towels she'd been carrying, lifting him in her arms, clutching him to her body. Mike dropped down beside his wife, hugging them both.

'Thank you,' Mike said, looking at both Alex and Isobella. 'Thank you so much.'

'Oh, God, yes,' Theresa added rocking an inconsolable Sam in her arms. 'I don't know how it happened, but just—thank you...thank you for your seeing him, for finding him. I don't want to think about what could have happened—' She broke into a flurry of tears again.

'It's okay, love,' Mike said gruffly, hugging her tighter. 'Let's not drive ourselves crazy with what-ifs.'

Alex nodded. 'I'm just pleased we could be of assistance.'

They all sat in a dripping huddle for the next few minutes, watching anxiously as Sam's cries slowly subsided. Alex suggested they get him fully medically checked out when they landed on Temora, and Mike and Theresa were more than glad to follow his advice.

Sam sniffled and pointed to a seagull wheeling in the sky overhead. 'Birdie,' he said. The adults looked at him, stunned, and then roared with laughter at his intact innocence. Sam said 'birdie' again for good measure, obviously pleased by their cheery response.

'I don't think there's any lasting damage with him.' Alex smiled, ruffling Sam's wet locks as the little boy yawned.

'He's no doubt exhausted,' Isobella murmured. Nothing like an interrupted nap and a hypoxic incident to induce fatigue.

Theresa stood, aided by Mike, and Isobella and Alex followed suit. 'I think I'll put him down for a nap and stay with him,' she said, rubbing her nose against his.

Mike watched them go. 'Do you mind if I join them for a while? I promise I'll have you on Temora in plenty of time for your flight.'

'Of course not,' Alex said. 'Go, man. Go be with your little Houdini.'

Mike grinned at them and they watched him go. Alex turned back to Isobella, remembering the moment he'd seen her dive over the side, not knowing why, his heart in his mouth. 'That was an incredibly brave thing to do. It can't have been easy for someone with a water phobia.'

Isobella shrugged, her heart beating madly, her hands trembling as full realisation hit her. 'I guess I didn't have time to stop and think about it too much.'

She looked dazed and his brow creased. 'Are you okay?'

She nodded briskly. 'Well, maybe a little wet, but…'

Alex laughed, his gaze drawn to her dripping hair and then down further to her now very see-through shirt. He could see she was wearing the cream bra with the butterfly at her cleavage he'd spied that first day on Piccolo. He knew he shouldn't, but his gaze moved further south, anticipating a peek at the matching knickers.

But his gaze didn't get quite that far. The shirt was plastered to her abdomen, and he blinked at what he saw there. A mass of purple whip-like marks blemishing her flat stomach. Very like a *Fleckeri* scar. Very, *very* like.

He stared as his heart pounded in his chest. 'Is that what I think it is?'

Alex's gravelly voice sounded almost steely, and his cerulean eyes were flecked with chips of ice. Isobella shivered. She looked down, shocked to discover her thin white cotton shirt was completely transparent—she might as well have been wearing nothing. She crossed her arms across her abdomen. 'Alex—'

He batted her arms away, his hands holding them locked by her sides. Blood roared in his head. 'Show me.'

The husky demand brooked no argument.

Their gazes clashed as her arms railed against the restraints of his. 'Alex.'

'Show me.'

He was looking at her intently, and her breath suddenly became ragged. Quite unexpectedly the moment had turned into something else entirely. She was very aware of him as a man, with all that brooding intensity focused solely on her. His hands grazing her waist were sending hot needles of desire up to her breasts and down to her thighs. She felt small and vulnerable, defenceless in his grasp. He was angry, and it shouldn't be turning her on, but she found herself strangely aroused.

The sea lapped the sides of the anchored boat, loud in a tense silence as vast as the ocean around them. It bobbed gently, their bodies rising and falling with the sway.

'Please, Alex.' Her voice stuttered into the electric space between them.

Alex couldn't bear the raw appeal in her voice. Nausea surged through his system at the mere thought that her body might have fallen victim to the searing brand of a box jellyfish. He'd listened to too many victim horror stories. The thought that she had been through such an ordeal was too awful to contemplate.

Isobella saw the flexing movement at the angle of his jaw. Felt the barely leashed power in the tightening of the bands around her wrists. Without any warning he grabbed the two edges of her shirt and ripped them apart, buttons scattering to the edges of the deck.

Isobella gasped. 'Alex!'

He ignored her, his gaze rapidly seeking the marks he was all too familiar with. His breath hissed out as he took in the magnitude of her scars, horrified by the extent of them. Rivulets of water beaded her skin, pearling on the flat planes of her abdomen, pooling in the shallow recess of her belly button. He didn't notice.

Nor did he notice the transparency of her underwear, the visibility of her erect nipples or the dark patch at the front of her satin knickers. He had eyes only for the damage, for the ugly purple brands left by the tentacles as they had fired their deadly poison into her beautiful body. His gaze raked her stomach with clinical intensity. Her long, lean torso was completely covered, from the ribs down to beyond the band of her pants.

Things suddenly became clearer. Her dislike of the ocean. The way she hid herself away. The startling empathy she'd shown him. And Danielle. The Isobella Nolan phenomena was suddenly making sense.

'Isobella,' he whispered, his gaze flicking momentarily to her face.

He noticed the trachey scar for the first time, and another piece of the puzzle fell in place. All those high-necked shirts. That god-awful bow. His eyes returned to her abdomen, unable to look away.

Isobella's breath heaved in and out. She was speared to the spot by his brutal inspection. She stood before him, more vulnerable, more exposed than she'd been in her life. More than she'd ever been modelling lingerie on a Paris catwalk. More than three weeks in Intensive Care. More than the other night, when she'd been practically naked and he'd been deep inside her.

But she couldn't move. It was like that moment again—the moment when the *Fleckeri* had attacked and the pain had been so intense that for a few seconds she'd been completely paralysed. Unable to scream, to move, to get away, to seek help.

His gaze rooted her to the spot. Warmth suffused her face. A breeze blew, chilling her wet

skin despite the heat of the day and his incendi-
ary stare. She was laid bare, and absolutely incapable of doing anything about it.

Alex groped behind him for the moulded
bench that lined the sides of the cruiser and sat
down heavily. 'Oh, my God.' He raked his hands
through his hair and then reached out to trace the
whip-like blemishes.

She saw shock furrow his brow, a look of
horror tauten his full lips, and Isobella's brain
finally switched on. She recoiled from his touch.
'No!' Hot tears stung her eyes as she turned her
back to him, desperately pulling together the
edges of her ruined shirt.

'They're… They're…' He groped for an apt
description.

'Hideous,' she finished for him, as she
whipped around, her fingers worrying the edges
of the shirt together at her throat.

Alex blinked at her vehemence, his brain still
grappling with what he'd just seen. He noticed
the familiar movement of her hand to her throat
and realised it wasn't a nervous gesture, as he'd
originally assumed. 'No!' he denied vehemently.

'And yet you look at me as if I have a disease
you're going to catch,' she spat. Anthony had

done exactly the same thing. Before he had run. At least she'd had one night of blind passion when her body had been revered by Alex. She looked around for the sarong she'd discarded before her leap into the ocean.

Alex ran a hand through his hair. 'No. I'm just…in shock.' Her scars were by far the most extensive he'd ever seen. 'I look at them and I can't even begin to imagine the pain…the trauma you must have been through. But then I look at them and clinically…they're fascinating.'

Isobella bit down on her tongue to stop more tears welling in her eyes. First he looked at her as if she was contagious, and then like a specimen under a microscope in one of his labs.

She gave a short, derisive laugh. 'To think men used to look at me with yearning. Do you know how many magazines this body sold?'

Alex stood, her words sinking in, her identity finally dawning on him. 'Oh, my God—you're *her*. You're Izzy. Izzy Tucker. The model. The one who was stung on a beach off Cardwell during a photo shoot. The one we've been looking for.'

Well, give the man a cigar. 'The very same.'

She located her sarong and tied it tight around her waist, using it to keep her shirt together.

He took a step towards her. 'Why didn't you tell me?'

She took a step back. 'It was none of your business.'

She was in total flight now. Her secret had been discovered. And, like the wounded animal she was, she knew the best form of defence was attack. She needed to push him back behind the line they'd crossed.

Alex felt frustration surge through his system. 'You knew I was keen to talk to you.'

Attack. Attack. 'I didn't want to talk to *you.*'

'Not even after the other night?' Hadn't they shared something special? Something meaningful? It hadn't just been sex. They both knew it.

Attack. Attack. 'You think because I slept with you I owe you my life story?'

Alex's jaw clenched. She made it sound cheap. 'I told you mine.' He had laid himself bare in a way that he hadn't in years. And to a woman too. He didn't do that. He wouldn't have done that if he hadn't felt some connection with her. A level of trust that he'd never experienced with another woman. Not even Sonya.

Isobella couldn't refute his words. His candour had surprised her. Humbled her, even. She'd known it hadn't been easy for him to open up to her that way. 'This isn't a competition.'

He ignored her. 'Was that what the nightmare was about? Do you have bad dreams about the day it happened to you?' He remembered how frightened she'd been, how she had trembled against him as fragile as a newborn kitten.

'I'm fine,' she dismissed evasively.

One thing he knew for sure—she wasn't fine. And he knew that somewhere deep in her heart of hearts she must know it too. She was hiding herself away. Shying away from life. Why else was she pushing *him* away so hard? She'd let him catch a glimpse of the woman she really was. Passionate and sexy and unguarded. He couldn't bear to think of her going back to being a lab recluse.

'You're not fine. You're a mess. Hiding your body and your beauty in baggy clothes and ugly glasses, shutting yourself away in the secluded environment of a lab.'

'Hey, I'll deal with my issues my way.'

'By avoiding them?' he asked incredulously.

No one had ever called her on the way she had

coped. Not even her sister. Isobella wasn't about to hear it from someone who up until a week ago had been a long-distance crush, a sexy voice down the telephone line. 'I don't think people who live in glass houses should throw stones,' she said acidly. 'At least I'm hurting no one but myself. You? You're branding the entire female sex as untrustworthy because one woman screwed you over.'

She made a fair point. 'Maybe not any more. What happened between us the other night…and this…' he gestured to her stomach '…it changes everything. Maybe I want more now.'

Isobella couldn't believe what she was hearing. Suddenly his faith in women had been restored because he'd slept with an employee and found a long-lost link to some valuable data? Or was it simpler than that?

'Why?' she demanded.

Because her scars had shown him how vulnerable she really was and he just couldn't bear it. She worked her butt off trying to prove her competence, prove her detachment, when underneath it all she was flesh and blood. A real woman. As susceptible to destiny and life's rocky road as everyone else.

He shook his head. 'I don't know.' He didn't know. He just knew he didn't want to go to back to Melbourne and never see her again. 'I can't explain... The thought of what you've been through...the pain and the fear... I feel like I need to...want to look after...protect...'

Isobella couldn't believe what she was hearing. Alex was standing before her, saying words she doubted he'd ever said to a woman. She let herself wallow in a brief fantasy that it was actually something other than a by-product of disbelief and misplaced macho paternalism.

'Why? Because you pity me? What's wrong? You can't catch-kiss-and-throw-back poor maimed Isobella?' she said scornfully. 'Well, let me tell you, Alexander Zaphirides, I was doing just fine before you came along, and I'll do just fine when you leave. I don't need your charity. I liked my life. I knew what I was doing. All you've done is mess it up.'

'Right then, let's get you folks to Temora,' Mike interrupted, his head and then the rest of his body appearing from the cabin.

He handed them each a large beach towel, obviously still too preoccupied with Sam's near-death episode to pay any heed to the knife-edge tension on deck. 'Theresa thought you might need to dry off.'

Alex could have strangled Mike for choosing that particular moment to come back, and he watched Isobella withdraw, wrapping the thick towel around her, cloaking herself from his questions, shielding herself from the world again. He hadn't meant to insult her by implying that she couldn't fend for herself. But something was happening inside him. Something was twisting in his gut. And it was telling him she wasn't like anyone he'd ever known.

And his fishing days were over.

CHAPTER TEN

ISOBELLA headed for a restroom as soon as she stepped foot in the air-conditioned haven of Cairns Airport. She discarded her ripped shirt and sarong in the bin and climbed into much more suitable shapeless trousers and baggy shirt. The usual buzz of gratification that hummed through her system as she covered up failed to materialise.

But she was fully covered, and she patted her throat reassuringly as she inspected her reflection in the mirror through her bookish glasses. She admired her armour, and for the first time since Alex had ripped off her shirt felt confident of repelling any arguments he might throw her way.

All she had to do was sit through the next two hours and then she would never need to see Alex again. The things that had happened today and the other night could not be undone. But they could be forgotten. And the sooner her Greek-god boss was out of sight, the sooner he could be out of mind.

Alex was already waiting in his seat when she boarded the plane, and the look he gave her as he took in her Isobella-esque appearance was faintly amused. 'Do you think I'm going to forget what lies beneath all those layers?'

Isobella shivered at the low growl directed towards her ear as she sat down and buckled up. She could have almost forgiven him had he been referring to her naked body alone. But she knew without even having to ask that it was her scars he was alluding to. How could he ever see the woman beneath now? And when had she started to care?

It was imperative she re-establish their professional relationship. 'I don't think anything. I expect you to realise this is none of your business and act like my boss.'

Alex heard the crispness in her voice. 'I think we blurred that line on Piccolo, don't you?'

Isobella felt the pull down low in her pelvis as the scrape of his voice momentarily sucked her back into the sensual vortex of that night. 'I think we can both agree that what happened the other night was a mistake.'

Alex's first instinct was to protest, but of course she was right. It shouldn't have happened. He was her boss, they'd been there on business, and she'd been vulnerable. But they both knew there'd been a force greater than themselves at work that night. Greater even than the cyclone that had raged outside. 'I wish all my mistakes felt that bad.'

'Alex. You agreed we would act like it never happened. If this is going to be an issue between us then I'll just have to resign.'

Isobella held her breath. She couldn't believe the threat that had slipped from her mouth. She loved her job. She believed in what they were doing and had complete faith that they would ultimately discover a substance that would dramatically improve the scarring endured by *Fleckeri* victims. And she wanted to be there when they did. Hell, she wanted to be *the one* who did.

Alex frowned. She was looking at him with a cool, serious look in those deadly brown eyes. The thought of her working elsewhere, at another lab for someone else, was highly disturbing. She was one of his best researchers, after all. It would be bad business practice to let her walk away. And Dr Alexander Zaphirides hadn't built up a medical research empire by making bad business decisions.

He sighed. 'Of course.'

Isobella nodded, letting out the breath that was now stretching her lungs to breaking point. She calmly turned back to face the chair in front, pulled out the in-flight magazine and flipped it open to a random page. She could feel Alex's gaze boring into her temple, and her hand trembled slightly with the effort it took to appear unaffected.

The plane taxied to the runway and the head stewardess made the usual announcements. The aircraft lifted into the endless blue sky and soon after lunch was served.

'Dr Zaphirides—so nice to see you again, sir. Can I get you a drink?'

Isobella felt her jaw clench as Red stood beside her, oozing charm and sex appeal all over the aisle. She didn't look up from her reading material.

Alex saw Isobella's knuckles tighten on the pages of the magazine. He smiled at the stewardess. 'Thank you, that would be marvellous. I might have a Scotch and ice.' *Damn, the woman was driving him to drink.*

'And you, ma'am?'

Isobella didn't think for a minute that Red gave two hoots whether she wanted a drink or not. 'No, thank you,' she said politely, not bothering to look up from what she was reading. She didn't want to see the look of lust in the other woman's eyes, the sexual confidence. How good would it feel to be able to look at a man and know you could have him?

Alex's drink arrived, and Red lingered to flirt outrageously for a while. Isobella endured it and Alex's equally flirty banter with as much indifference as she could muster.

'Can I ask you something?' Alex asked Isobella as he finished his meal, passing her his untouched bread roll.

Isobella took the roll, ignoring the rub of his husky voice all the way down her spine. 'No.'

Alex chuckled, watching her break the bread open with her fingers and slather it with butter. 'It's not about Piccolo. I promise.'

Isobella bit into the roll. 'All right, then,' she acquiesced grudgingly. He had shared his leftovers, after all.

He watched her bite into the roll. A smear of butter glistened on her bottom lip, and sinful thoughts of removing it with his own slithered through his mind before she flicked her tongue out to clear it off. It took him a moment or two to remember what he'd been about to say.

'Why do you hide your body?'

Isobella swallowed, almost choking on the last of the bread roll. She stared at him, the urge to deny it strong. But he already knew too much about her. Lying seemed pointless. 'Why do you think?' she asked caustically.

He shrugged, dismayed at the bitterness in her voice. 'I honestly don't know. You don't need to wear baggy clothes to cover your scars. Any shirt's going to do that.'

Isobella blinked. He didn't get it. He truly didn't get it. She was dismayed to feel tears gathering in her eyes. How could she explain to him how deeply the mental scars had wounded her? 'They're hideous, Alex.'

Her voice was tremulous, and she was looking at him as if he'd grown another head. As if he'd never understand in a million years. But he did understand. Some. He knew what it was like to be travelling along a path only to have the signposts change on you. 'No, Isobella. They're not.'

She looked at him askance. 'How can you say

that? You saw them. They're…they're ugly…repulsive, revolting.'

'No. They're not,' he repeated calmly.

Isobella was blown away by the steady honesty in his open blue gaze. She looked away. She was too desperate to believe what he was saying. Too vulnerable after their recent confrontation to be strong. She would not let his pretty words persuade her into ignoring the evidence of her own eyes and that of the two men who were supposed to have loved her.

'Well, maybe you can look at them differently. With the calm, clinical eye of a physician. No doubt you find them *fascinating*. But, trust me, other men don't.'

Alex heard the stiffness in her voice masking what was obviously deep-seated hurt. He shrugged. 'Some men are too stupid to live.'

Isobella was so surprised by his honesty and his matter-of-fact delivery that she laughed, despite the whirl of anxiety cramping her insides.

Alex watched as the laughter petered out from her face and doubt drew her brows together. 'What was his name?'

She hesitated. 'Paolo.'

Alex nodded, and waited for her to elaborate.

'He was…is…he still is a photographer. He freelances for all the top fashion magazines.' She remembered seeing his name only a few months ago in a *Vogue* spread she'd been admiring. 'He was shooting that day sixteen years ago…I collapsed at his feet.' She felt the pain all over again. From the searing bite of the tentacles and from Paolo's rejection.

Alex could see the distance in her gaze and could tell she was back at that day. He waited for her to say more, but it didn't look as if she was coming back any time soon. 'He…left you? After?' he prodded gently.

She nodded, coming out of her reverie. 'He couldn't even bear to look at me.'

Alex reached for her hand and covered it with his own. He felt her flinch, but held on anyway. He remembered her telling him it had been a long time since she'd had sex. Had it been sixteen years? 'There's been no one else?'

'There was another man. A couple of years later. I thought he might be special. He was nuts about me…apparently. But he…he ran pretty quickly when he saw the *real* me.'

Alex squeezed her hand. Some men really

were too stupid to live. 'You lost a lot that day on the beach. Your lover. Your career.'

Yes, she had. But it wasn't just that—she'd lost her sense of self that day. Her perception of who she was. But how did she explain that? She couldn't.

'No. Not my career. It was my last shoot. I was retiring from modelling.'

Alex raised an eyebrow. 'Oh?'

'I was sick of the industry. I'd been modeling since the age of six.'

Alex's eyebrows practically hit his hairline. *'Six?'*

Isobella nodded. 'Catalogue stuff to begin with—you know, department store adverts, children's clothing, that kind of thing. I did my first catwalk job on my twelfth birthday. I was fourteen my first season in Paris.'

'That's a long time. A lot to turn your back on. From what I understand of your case you were on your way to supermodel status.'

Isobella nodded, looking at their entwined hands resting in her lap. 'I know it sounds really glamorous…and it was. But there was so much pressure to stay thin. And not just within a normal healthy weight range, but stick-insect-thin. I was tired of being obsessed with it. I just wanted to…eat a doughnut without worrying about the calories. Although I was lucky. I have a great metabolism—'

Alex laughed. 'I noticed.'

Isobella blushed. *So? She liked to eat.*

'Too many girls I modelled with suffered from eating disorders. Some of them used drugs to stay thin. I didn't want to head down that path. Modelling can mess with your head. It's hard to explain. It's such a superficial world—a goldfish bowl. You feel like a slab of meat in a market. Every flaw, every blemish, every extra pound, every stray zit is a black mark against you. A risk of losing a job to another girl.'

Alex shook his head. 'No wonder you're so screwed-up about your body.'

She opened her mouth to protest. But what could she say? She *was* screwed up about it. She moved her hand out from under his. 'You have to understand, Alex. I strutted the catwalks of Paris and Milan. I graced the cover of practically every fashion magazine in the world. I went from beautiful swan to ugly duckling in one searingly painful minute. That's not the way it's supposed to go, Alex. It's not supposed to work in reverse.'

Alex couldn't believe what he was hearing. 'You're *alive*, Isobella. Do you know how close you came to dying? I've read your notes. You had three cardiac arrests in those first two days. If they hadn't had an ambulance on site at the beach that day you would have died on the sand.'

The thought was utterly repugnant to him. Even thinking about her lying on the beach as her life force ebbed, relying on strangers to pound on her chest and pull her back from the brink, made him ill.

'And I live with the ugly reminder every day.'

Didn't she understand how lucky she was? 'Why does the scarring matter? You just told me you were leaving modeling anyway.'

Isobella looked at him incredulously. 'It *matters*,' she choked out. 'It changed everything. Everything I thought I was—thought I knew about me… It changed my entire perception of myself. Yes, I'd chosen to do something else with my life, but Izzy the model—that's still who I was, deep down. Then suddenly I'm scarred. Blemished. Flawed.'

'So this whole shapeless clothes thing—it's not just about covering your scars, is it? It's about hiding from the world because you're not

Izzy any more. Pretending that whole other you didn't even exist. You're letting it define you.'

She shied away from the brutal honesty of his words. She wanted to get up and walk away, open the door and never look back, but sucking two hundred passengers to their doom wasn't going to make the truth any easier to bear.

'How can it not?' she demanded. 'People's life experiences do define them. Your cancer did. It made you change direction. Switch specialties.'

'Yes, but I'm not hiding what happened to me. Pretending it didn't. Pretending I'm someone else. I'm not letting it affect who I am.'

Isobella looked at his neck scars, open for everyone to see, and was overwhelmed by the urge to trace them with her finger. No, he wasn't pretending. At least not about what had happened to him. But…

'You close yourself off to women, to any sort of meaningful relationship, because Sonya walked away from you.'

Alex felt the needle from her accurate dig prick at his conscience. 'That's not the same thing.'

'Isn't it?'

No, damn it, it wasn't. And they weren't talking about *him*. 'You've let this thing shape every aspect of your life. You've let it make you a total recluse. You didn't just change direction, you stuck yourself into reverse, backed yourself into the garage and threw away the key. You've let it completely take over your life.'

His words cut her with their razor-sharp insight. What the hell would he know? 'You don't know me,' she murmured.

'Maybe I know you better than you think.'

She shook her head mutinously. 'If you did you'd know that any changes I made, I made because I wanted to. I was sick of being Izzy. Sick of the superficial lifestyle. The attack just ensured I completely ditched all the Izzy trappings. There are way more important things in life than what shoes and bag go best with a Chanel jacket, you know? I'm happy with my life. I'm happy with the lab and my job and, yes, with my awful glasses and baggy clothes. I don't need anything else in my life.'

Alex dropped his head close to her ear. 'You're a liar,' he murmured.

Isobella sucked in a breath at the erotic slither of his husky accusation. 'No. I *am* happy,' she insisted.

'I saw your underwear strewn all over the bed at Piccolo. Your very…sexy underwear.'

His tone dropped another notch, and she shivered as she thought about him looking at her personal things. Touching her silk and lace as he had her bra and knickers the night of the cyclone. She should have been affronted, but his scratchy voice and the heat of her memories were weaving their way through her pelvic floor muscles, tightening each one as it fluttered by.

'You may think you want to forget about being a woman, a sexy woman with a woman's needs, but your lingerie says different. Your lingerie says *I am woman. Hear. Me. Purr.*'

Isobella swallowed. Her underwear was the only concession to femininity, to her past life, she had allowed herself. He wasn't supposed to see it. No one was supposed to know. It was her guilty little secret.

'You want to know how else I know how desperately you want to be that woman you're suppressing? When I was inside you, deep inside you, there was no façade, Isobella. You let go of all that stuff. All those inhibitions. You were *all* woman.'

Isobella blushed, remembering her complete abandon. 'It was dark,' she muttered. And she had wanted him. It had been a heady combination.

Alex frowned down at her. 'What's that got to do with it?'

Isobella snorted. 'You think you would have been so eager the other night if you could have seen me? Seen my sc—my body? What I really looked like?'

Ah. He looked at her. She was tearing her napkin to pieces in her lap and she looked deadly serious. 'If you think for a minute your scarring turns me off then you're crazy.'

She heard the absolute certainty in his voice, and then remembered how clinically he had looked at her abdomen—as if she'd been under a microscope. 'Oh, no,' she said, trying to keep the bitterness out of her voice. 'I'm sure they're highly *fascinating* for you.'

Alex realised he'd made a critical error when he'd examined her so thoroughly on the boat. He thought for a moment, then pursed his lips and pushed them right up close to her ear.

'You are sexy. Your body in those awful clothes and horrible glasses is sexy. Your naked body is a whole other level sexy. In fact I want nothing more than to take you into the nearest bathroom, rip those dreadful clothes off you and show you just how very much I don't give a damn about how fascinating those scars are.'

Isobella froze, the fingers plucking at her napkin stilling at his sinful proposition. The brush of his lips rendered her incapable of movement. 'You can't mean that,' she whispered.

'I do. I absolutely do,' he whispered back.

Red came along just then and reached across Isobella, collecting Alex's tray. 'I hope everything was satisfactory, Dr Zaphirides?' she purred.

Isobella didn't hear Alex's reply. Her brain was sluggish, stupefied by desire. She felt as if her skull had been flipped open and an electric mixer had been applied to her brain, scrambling it into a million pieces. He thought she was sexy? Dared she believe him?

Like Paolo? He had told her how sexy she was about a hundred times a day. And a bunch of other fashion industry people had used the word as casually as if it were a preposition. Anthony had kissed and touched her at every opportunity in their briefly intense month, had told her he was the luckiest man alive.

Why should she believe it from Alex? Even though his cerulean gaze was hypnotically honest and his frank words free from artifice? She wanted to believe him. But wanting didn't make it so. Why should she put her faith in a catch-kiss-and-throw-back man? Even if his words were sincere, he was never going to commit to her. She knew where he stood on that. But, after years of being alone and pretending it didn't matter, she wanted more than a casual affair.

'Where were we?' Alex murmured, after the stewardess had moved off.

Isobella sat up straighter in the chair, steeling herself to deliver a stern lecture. Fortunately the head stewardess made the 'prepare for descent' announcement—asking passengers to fasten seatbelts, place trays up, return seats to the upright position.

'Landing, I do believe,' Isobella said coolly.

'Isobella, I think we were in the middle of something.'

'No, Alex.' She looked him straight in the eye. 'We weren't.'

Alex saw determination solidify her gaze, as hard as year-old toffee, before she turned away from him and reclaimed her in-flight magazine. She wanted to be left alone. That much was clear. She wanted him to butt out and leave her to her lonely lab geek life. This was none of his business, and she redefined complicated.

He didn't do complicated. He liked simple. Easy. Carefree. And, no matter how unappealing they all sounded right now, he'd grant her wish. He'd leave her alone, stop interfering, get the hell back to Melbourne and his uncomplicated life.

But he did make a mental note to visit the Brisbane lab more frequently.

CHAPTER ELEVEN

ISOBELLA peered down her microscope at the latest tentacular material from a *Fleckeri* Mike and Theresa had sent to the lab yesterday. Her mind wandered to Alex standing on the beach the morning after the cyclone, his white shirt flapping in the breeze. He'd looked so sexy, so vital and male.

Damn it! One month down the track and Isobella finally admitted what she'd known almost from her first day back. She was going to have to resign. She was in love with her boss and being back at the lab was a daily torturous reminder of it.

In love with Dr Alexander Zaphirides.

How stupid!

He was everywhere. Not just in her head. He was on her e-mail and her phone line, and in the conversations she overheard from her colleagues. It was his lab. Every piece of equipment, every piece of paper had his name on it. Everywhere there were constant reminders of him.

She couldn't think. She couldn't sleep. She was distracted, and flitted from being irritable one moment to being daydreamy the next. Her productivity had slipped. She'd stare at a specimen for ages before remembering what she was supposed to be doing with it. Her data entry was slow. She forgot where she put things and planning her day was hopeless. Her colleagues were noticing.

And then, when she'd finally get it together, Alex would ring. With his sinful voice. Oh, sure, it was always about work, but he'd manage to slip in something seemingly innocent about Piccolo, and then suddenly she'd be back there— back to that night, with him inside her, chasing the storm and her fears away, whispering to her, his voice stroking her body like an extra hand.

And if that wasn't enough he was redefining her role—using Reg's absence to get her out of the lab to do more field work. She'd been out and done follow-ups on several old *Fleckeri* cases in the Brisbane region twice already, and he'd sent her an e-mail yesterday with an airline ticket in the attachment for another follow-up.

She knew what he was doing. He was determined to get her out of the lab. Out of her comfort zone. If only he knew that it didn't matter any more. The lab was no longer her refuge. Everything in it reminded her of him. Her haven was no longer. Nowhere was safe from thoughts of Alex.

She waited till everyone had left for the evening and dialled Alex's direct line. The temptation to e-mail him her resignation had been strong, but she knew she owed him a more personal explanation.

She glanced at the time. Six o'clock. She knew he'd be there. He was an even bigger workaholic than she was. She mentally ran through her speech as her foot tapped an agitated rhythm on the floor, waiting for him to pick up.

'Hello?'

Isobella's prepared speech died in her throat at the decidedly normal, decidedly girlie voice that answered the phone.

'Er…hello? Who's this?' Isobella asked, frowning at the phone. Surely she hadn't rung the wrong extension? She knew Alex's number by heart.

'It's Sonya Nikolaidis.'

Isobella froze, her hand tightening convulsively around the receiver. She heard Alex in the background, asking who it was. She stared at the phone for a second before dropping it back in its cradle as if it had burnt her.

Alex and Sonya?

She swallowed, feeling sick. And stupid. And foolish. She'd been mooning over him like a teenager. Unable to forget their time and what had happened. Reliving it again and again like a pathetic lovesick sap. While he'd been back in the game. How many women had he slept with this past four weeks? How many nibbles on his line?

She sat at her computer and composed a quick, brief and professional letter of resignation. She attached it to a one-line e-mail and clicked 'send' before she changed her mind. Then she switched off her computer and left the lab without a backward glance.

Alex had a hangover the next morning when he opened the e-mail. He'd been drinking too much lately, and after his meeting with Sonya to secure further monies from MediCorp he'd imbibed more than he should have. It rankled to have to deal with her on a professional basis.

He read the e-mail through bleary eyes. Isobella was resigning? Effective after Reg came back to work and was settled back in?

What the—?

'Over my dead body,' he muttered as he dialled her number. He needed her in Brisbane, damn it. She was practically running the project single-handed.

'Trop Med—this is Isobella.'

Alex could have reached through the phone as her cheery greeting jangled through his aching head. 'I don't accept.'

Isobella gripped the phone hard. 'Alex.'

'What's the meaning of this?' he demanded.

'It's all in the e-mail.'

Alex's top lip curled. The letter was textbook. It told him nothing. 'It's rubbish, Isobella. I thought you were dedicated to the project? I thought it was the most important thing in your life? The centre of your universe?'

It had been. But now her love for him took pole position. 'I don't have to give you any reasons, Dr Zaphirides.'

'The hell you don't.' First she slept with him,

and then she told him to forget it had ever happened, and then she resigned? One of his best researchers?

'I'm not going to leave you in the lurch, Dr Zaphirides. I'll wait until Reg has resumed full duties. It'll give you plenty of time to find a re-placement.'

Replacement? God damn it, he didn't want someone else. He wanted her.

'I'm flying to Brisbane today.' He scanned his diary looking at what he could postpone or cancel. 'This afternoon. I'll book a table at Daniel's. I'll pick you up at seven.'

She did not want to have dinner with him. Even if Daniel's was one of the poshest restaurants in Brisbane. She certainly didn't want him picking her up. 'You don't even know where I live,' she said exasperatedly.

'You forget, Isobella, I'm the boss. I know everything.'

His gravelled voice left her in no doubt that he was thinking of all the things he knew about her. *Even the things he shouldn't.* She swallowed. 'Dr Zaphirides—'

'I swear to God, Isobella, if you call me Dr Zaphirides one more time…'

Isobella shivered as the husky threat hung in the air. She sighed. 'It won't make any difference, Alex.'

'It's not a request, Isobella.'

She bristled at his autocratic statement, and remembered how he had presented her with the Piccolo *fait accompli* in much the same manner. She'd forgotten in all her mooning how determined he could be.

Alex waited for a response, unsure as to why he was being so hard-nosed. All he knew was she couldn't leave. 'Isobella. I think you owe me a face-to-face on this.'

She knew he was right. Whether she wanted to ignore it or not, they were more than acquaintances, more than just colleagues. *She loved him, for God's sake!*

It was on the tip of her tongue to ask whether Sonya would be joining them, but she bit down hard to prevent the green-eyed monster having its way.

'Fine,' she snapped, and banged the phone down in his ear.

Alex smiled despite his annoyance. There were very few employees who would hang up on him. But then Isobella wasn't a run-of-the-mill employee. For a start he didn't know any of his other workers so intimately, and nor did he want to. And there wasn't one of them he'd fight this hard to keep. Not when they so patently wanted to go.

Somehow telling himself it was all about her research skills just wasn't washing. Maybe it was the thought that she was ruining all his plans. Having her in Brisbane had been perfect. She was near, but not too close. He could be in contact, make subtle changes, force her out of hiding under the guise of the job and slowly bring her out of her shell.

He could see her regularly, check on her progress, slowly insinuate himself into her life. Maybe eventually coax her into a date or two. And then a repeat performance of what had happened on Piccolo. God knew, he hadn't been able to think of anything else for weeks.

Frankly, it was a damn nuisance that she'd decided not to play the game. Alexander Zaphirides was a man who did not like his plans interfered with.

When Isobella opened the door to Alex promptly at seven he knew instantly he'd been wrong. It hadn't been about her work, or about keeping her close so he could chip away at her shell. He was in love with her. It was as simple as that. She was fresh-faced and lovely and he wanted to fall into her eyes and drown in them for ever.

'Come in,' she invited stiffly, clenching her fists to stop herself from reaching for the broad expanse of his magnificent chest in his exquisitely cut suit jacket. Dear God, she had missed him. 'I'll just get my purse,' she said, turning on her heel.

Alex wandered into the apartment in a daze, his revelation making him dizzy. He noticed nothing about where she lived, or the things she surrounded herself with. He was too busy castigating himself for his blindness. How could he not have seen he'd fallen in love with her?

Maybe because it wasn't an emotion with which he was overly acquainted. He'd certainly never felt this overwhelming sense of rightness with Sonya. He'd felt lust and possession and pride, but never this buzz energising every cell with a delicious ache to have her by his side always.

He turned to face her as he heard her approaching. She strode towards him and he blinked. In his tailspin he hadn't noticed her attire. She was wearing a dress. A magnificent dress.

The shapeliness of her long coltish legs was clearly evident as the clingy burgundy fabric hugged their outline. As was everything else. Her breasts were outlined in all their pert, perfect glory. And the material clung to the flatness of her stomach before flaring gently from thigh level down to the hem that swung around her knees.

The dress was sleeveless, baring her beautiful shoulders and nicely toned arms to his view. The V neckline rested on the generous rise of her cleavage. Her neck was bare, her trachey scar exposed.

Sans glasses, her face was classically beautiful. Her glossed lips so very, very kissable. His ugly duckling had become a beautiful swan.

'Isobella.'

She could hear the hiss of his breath, and the way her name was torn raggedly from his damaged cords. What had possessed her to wear the dress she wasn't sure. In fact she hadn't been sure about wearing it at all. Still wasn't.

It had gone to Cairns and back with her unworn—why had she felt the urge to change her mind at the last minute tonight and slip it over her head? Maybe it had been Sonya's voice on Alex's phone last night, goading her. Maybe at this, their last hurrah, she wanted to show him she could compete with his ex.

But the way he was looking—no, gaping—made her nervous, and she squirmed beneath his silent scrutiny, her hand nervously stroking her very exposed neck. She wanted to flee back to the safety of her bedroom and seek solace in her standard clothes. Remove her contacts, push her glasses on. Climb into the baggy trousers and shapeless top she'd laid out on her bed.

She wasn't used to men staring at her any more. What on earth had possessed her to wear this dress? 'It's…it's not appropriate,' she stuttered into the growing silence. She swallowed against a throat that felt as if it had been lined with cement. 'I'll go and change.' And she whirled on her heel and bolted for her bedroom.

Alex blinked at the apparition that had disappeared as rapidly as it had appeared. What the—? 'Isobella? Wait!' he called after her, following her escape.

Isobella shut and locked her door, sagging against it. What had she been thinking? It didn't matter how much she dressed up the outside, he'd already seen what she really looked like. Tears welled in her eyes and she blinked hard, refusing to let them fall. Who had she been trying to kid? Yes, he'd told her she was sexy, but he'd been with Sonya since then.

Beautiful.

Greek.

Unblemished.

Perfect.

She moved away from the door, pulling the dress up over her head and hurling it on the ground in disgust. The door handle twisted suddenly, startling her. It was followed by a loud thumping and she grabbed her robe. 'Go away, Alex,' she choked, the tears fighting to get past her determination not to cry.

Her voice was muffled, but he could hear the emotion straining it. 'Let me in.'

Isobella secured the tie around her waist and pulled the lapels tight against her throat. 'I don't want to talk to you, Alex. I never want to see you again,' she called.

'I swear to God, Isobella, I'm going to kick it down if you don't open it.'

Isobella stared at the door, scandalised. But she believed him. She looked down at her robe, knowing it wasn't the most suitable attire to be entertaining a gentleman in, but, hell—he'd seen her in a lot less. And he wouldn't be staying. She walked to the door and flipped the lock.

Alex took a calming breath before he entered. He was about to tell a woman who never wanted to see him again that he loved her. He opened the door cautiously, half expecting something to be hurled at his head. She was standing by the bed, her hand clutching her robe tight at her throat.

'Isobella.'

She darted him a nervous look, and he saw her knuckles tighten at her neck, but she didn't say anything—just stood looking mutinously at the floor.

His gaze fell on the discarded dress. 'Please get dressed and let's go to dinner.' His nerve had deserted him. She looked so closed-off right now. Maybe if he could get her to loosen up she'd be more receptive to what he had to say.

'I'm not going to dinner with you, Alex. It won't change the outcome. I'm resigning, and it doesn't matter what you say to try to persuade me—'

'Why?' he asked. 'Why do you want to leave? I thought you loved your job. And don't give me some politically correct legalese mumbo-jumbo.'

She did love her job. She *had*. But she loved

him more, and she just couldn't put herself through the torture of being so near to him and yet so far. He wanted her to be honest. But she couldn't. Not totally. She didn't want her heart to be crushed again—it might not survive this time.

'It's too hard now.'

Alex held his breath. 'Because of Piccolo?'

Isobella nodded.

Alex searched for words. The right words that might be the key to unlocking her guarded heart. 'You know, I learnt a lot about you while we were away. But I also learnt a lot about me. You told me that not all women are the same. That not all women leave. And I was actually starting to believe that. But here you are, walking away, because it's suddenly got too hard. Just like Sonya.'

Isobella felt a swelling in her chest, pushing at her ribs, grabbing at her heart, rising into her throat at the unfairness of his comparison. Sonya had cold-bloodedly left him when he had needed her most. It had been cruel and harsh and she *so* didn't deserve a second chance. The memory of Sonya's voice on Alex's phone line needled further.

She raised her head and looked him directly in

the eye. 'I would never have left you like she did,' she spat at him. 'Never.'

Alex saw the hard glitter in her gaze and the indignant rise of colour in her cheeks. He started to hope. His heart thumped a loud slow march in his chest. 'So why are you leaving me now?'

His husky voice growled at her, and she resented the hell out of his implication. He wasn't ill or dying. He didn't need her. That needled as well. 'I'm leaving you because I love you, not because I don't.'

Unlike Sonya.

There were a few moments of silence as her statement sank in. Isobella realised too late he'd goaded her into admitting the one thing she hadn't wanted him to know. She was frozen for a moment, frantically trying to organise her brain to take back what she'd said.

Alex couldn't believe what he'd heard. She loved him? Dared he hope it was true? It was more than he had dreamed possible. 'You love me?'

His voice was a mere whisper, and she could see the confusion in his gaze. Was he already trying to think of ways to reject her? To let her down gently? He took a step towards her.

'It's okay, Alex,' she said, holding out her hand

to ward him off as her heart broke—irreparably this time. She felt shaky all over, the earlier tears threatening again. 'I know you don't do this type of thing. I swear I didn't plan it or expect it. I know how you feel about relationships. I'll be out of your hair as soon as Reg comes back, and then you can forget all about me and this highly—' she sought around for a word '—distasteful conversation.'

Alex took three more steps and covered the distance between them, his heart tripping madly in his chest now. *She loved him.* 'Isobella,' he whispered, lifting his hand to cup her cheek, 'shut up.' And he lowered his eager mouth to her startled one.

Isobella felt a surge of desire blindside her as her lips clung to his of their own volition. She shouldn't be doing this, but he tasted as she remembered, and she'd been so hungry for him. Would it be so wrong to indulge for a little while? Just to get her through the lonely years ahead?

She ended the kiss with a fierce surge of passion. 'No.' She wrenched her mouth from his.

Alex breathed hard, staring into the murky

depths of her conflicted brown gaze. Her lips were moist from his attention and he wanted to be back there again, tasting her.

'I won't do this, Alex. I can't. I need more than a casual affair. I won't be just another fish to throw back when you're done with me.'

Alex smiled at her and rested his forehead against hers, trying to catch his breath and think. 'Good. Because I don't want you to go anywhere. I love you, Isobella. I want to marry you. I want you to be by my side for ever.'

Isobella shut her eyes, revelling in the erotic rub of his husky voice and the warmth of his breath on her face before wrenching herself away from him again. 'Don't play with me, Alex.'

Alex shook his head. 'I'm not. I love you. I mean it. I didn't realise it till I saw you again tonight, but it's true. I've been kidding myself into thinking that I needed you near because you're my top researcher. You needed to be brought out of your shell and I was just the man to do it. Thinking that I could eventually persuade you into having an affair with me. But I was lying to myself. I want more than that. I love you, Isobella. I want for ever. It's that simple.'

Simple? She gaped at him. How was for ever

simple? He had to be joking. The prospect of marriage, of for ever, had never entered her 'damaged goods' mentality. 'But…but how…? I mean what about…' How could someone so perfect, so beautiful, want someone so broken?

'Isobella.' Alex kissed her lips softly. He placed a hand over hers, still clutching her gown at her throat, and tugged at it gently. She resisted, and he kissed her mouth deep and slow again. He felt her grip loosen, and this time her hand fell away. He pulled away from her mouth as he eased the gown open at the neck.

Isobella felt the tears that had been threatening for a while well in her eyes as his mouth sought and found the scar at her neck. He kissed it tenderly. His hot tongue laving it lovingly.

Alex looked up to find tears glistening on her lashes. 'Hey,' he crooned, kissing them away. 'You're so beautiful, Isobella. So. Very. Beautiful.' He punctuated each word with a kiss. One to each eye, one on the tip of her little snub nose, and one on her upturned mouth.

Isobella didn't know what to say. She believed him. His honesty was like a beacon blazing from his cerulean eyes. 'Not as beautiful as Sonya,' she said wistfully.

Alex stilled. 'You have more beauty, more sincerity in your little finger, than Sonya possesses in her entire body. She did me the biggest favour the day she walked away. I must thank her for that.'

'You could have thanked her yesterday.'

Alex frowned.

'I rang. She answered.'

The hang-up? That had been Isobella? Was she…was she jealous? Alex smiled. 'I was negotiating a finance deal with MediCorp to continue the dermonecrosis research.'

'Ah.'

Alex tipped her chin, so she was looking at him and not at the knot of his tie. 'I don't want her, Isobella. I only want you. I'll only ever want you. Do you believe me?'

She gave a small nod.

'That doesn't look very convincing.'

Isobella shrugged. 'Why? Why do you want me? Over her? Over anyone else you could have? I'm totally messed up. I h…hate my scars. I can barely look at myself in the mirror. Hell, Alex, I don't even know if I can have babies.'

Alex shrugged, knowing that their relationship would have its challenges. 'We'll cross that bridge when we get to it.'

Isobella felt tears sting her eyes. 'I bet you Sonya can give you babies. Lots of little Greek babies, with golden skin and chubby cheeks.'

Alex chuckled. The jealousy in her voice was like music to his ears. 'I don't want Sonya's babies.'

'Well, you should—because you probably won't be having any with me.'

Alex sighed and placed his forehead against hers. 'Isobella.'

'No, Alex. *No*,' she said, partially moving out of his embrace. 'This is serious. I've seen you with kids. You're good. It's obvious you adore your nieces and nephews. You're a natural father.'

He shrugged. 'We'll adopt.'

Isobella shook her head. 'Face it, Alex, with my scars and my questionable fertility I'm… I'm…damaged goods.'

Alex's hand tightened around her waist. She might look like a fully-fledged swan tonight, but she still had an ugly duckling psyche he needed to break through. 'So am I. Do my scars turn you off? I hate my damaged voice too. Should I stop talking? Lock myself away? Become mute?'

Isobella started. To never hear the rub of his voice again would be a sin against nature. 'You…you don't like your voice?' she asked incredulously.

Alex shook his head. 'It's soft and scratchy. I used to have a voice that could freeze an intern at fifty paces. Now just raising it hurts. Why?' he asked, looking at her shaking her head at him as if he was talking utter drivel. 'Do you?'

Isobella gave a half-laugh, not quite able to believe that Alex had any insecurities, or that she was about to admit what she was about to admit. 'Oh, my Lord. All you have to do is open your mouth and I practically come on the spot.'

Alex blinked, momentarily shocked by her bald statement. And then he laughed. And kissed her hard on the mouth. He pulled away, winging one eyebrow. 'Really?'

Her head spun from the kiss as his sexy voice rumbled around her and her toes curled. *Drat the man.* Advantage Alex. 'Yes.' She blushed. 'Really.'

'Man, I can't wait to put that one to the test.'

She saw his look as he realized the power she had handed him on a platter and knew she was doomed. 'Seriously, Alex—'

Alex sighed and pulled back from her slightly. He reached out for the tie of her gown. 'May I?'

Isobella hesitated. She placed a hand over his. 'Please, Isobella. It'll be okay. I promise.'

She saw the sincerity shining from his eyes. He was asking her to trust him. Maybe it was time to take a leap of faith. Her hand fell away.

Alex felt his heart swell with love and pride. He knew what this was costing her. He pulled the tie and the belt came undone, the edges of her gown loosening. He knelt before her, his gaze never leaving her face as he slowly parted the material.

His hands came into contact with the warm skin of her abdomen and a gasp fell from her throat.

'It's okay,' he murmured, his eyes never leaving her face. He smoothed his hands over the flat planes of her stomach, resting them at the curve of her waist

He slowly looked away from her face, his gaze travelling down until he could see the purple marks branding her skin. He pressed a kiss to her stomach, just above her navel, and felt her muscles undulate beneath his lips, her hand burrow into his hair.

'I know you hate them,' he whispered against her skin, rubbing his nose, his mouth against the scars, kissing them lightly, laving them with his tongue as he had done her neck. 'But I love them—all of them.' He looked up at her. 'Because they brought you to me.'

Isobella felt more tears brim in her eyes, and she whimpered at the sensation of his mouth and the rumble of his voice against her stomach.

'I don't care if they mean we can't conceive. We'll take it one step at a time and we'll do what we have to do. Okay?' He looked up at her.

She nodded, her vision completely blurred, a lump choking her throat, making words impossible.

Alex turned his attention back to her belly, rubbing his cheek against the soft skin there. 'I would give anything to be able to go back to that day and stop what happened. Not because of these—' he stopped and kissed her stomach reverently '—but because the thought of you going through that experience, that pain, makes me physically ill.'

'Oh, Alex,' she murmured.

'These are a part of you. Part of who you are. And I wouldn't erase them even if I could. Let me show you. Let me spend my life showing you how much I worship your body. You helped me see that not all women are Sonyas. Helped me see that the love of one woman is far superior than the fancy of many. Let me help you see what a beautiful woman you still are.'

Isobella couldn't believe what she was hearing. The man she loved, loved her back. Accepted her, warts and all. Scarred, screwed-up and potentially infertile. What was she waiting for? Wasn't he the one she'd given up hope was even out there? The one who could see the swan beneath the duckling? The one she had never truly believed existed?

She swallowed against the ball of emotion choking her throat. 'Okay.'

Alex's lips stilled against her stomach as her voice reached him. He looked up. 'Really?'

She nodded through her tears. 'Really.'

He rose, his hands still holding firm around her bare midriff. He looked down into her face and stroked his thumb across her lips. He felt his loins stir as she whimpered, and followed his thumb with his lips. The stir became a leap as their tongues meshed.

'You don't really want to go out to dinner, do you?' he murmured some time later, coming up for air, his lips against her temple.

'I don't care if I never eat again,' she whispered.

Alex chuckled. 'Wow. It must be love.'

Isobella grinned at him and yanked his head down to prove it to him again and again.

EPILOGUE

THE sea lapped the shore of Piccolo Island in gentle licks as Isobella and Alex stood facing each other. The sun set in a blaze of gilded oranges behind them. Isobella wore a simple white sleeveless slip dress that hugged her figure with a plunging V-neckline. The hem fluttered around her bare ankles and the wet sand felt cool beneath her unshod feet.

Alex wore a white shirt, unbuttoned and flapping in the gentle sea breeze. It matched his white trousers. He also had bare feet.

'Do you take this woman to be your wife? To love her and take care of her all the days of your life?'

'I do. I absolutely do.'

Isobella grinned up at him, remembering how he had used those exact words to convince her how sexy she was on the plane. His unshaven face sported a scratchy three-day growth to match the erotic scratch of his voice, and the wind blew his hair across his head, tousling it in reckless abandon.

'And do you take this man to be your husband? To love him and take care of him all the days of your life?'

Alex waited for her words, still blown away that Isobella was his and willing to spend for ever with him. The red hibiscus in her hair complemented her dark toffee eyes and glorious high cheekbones.

'I do,' she whispered. 'I absolutely do.'

The celebrant smiled at them. 'Then, by the power vested in me, I declare you married. You may kiss.'

Isobella tossed away the posy of flowers she'd purchased at Temora and leapt into Alex's arms, locking her ankles around his waist and settling against the two strong arms that supported her bottom.

'Mrs Zaphirides,' he murmured, looking up at the excitement and love in her eyes.

'Mr Zaphirides.' She grinned, twining her arms around his neck and lowering her head for a kiss to seal their union.

Their first kiss as a married couple.

The first of many.

MEDICAL™

Large Print

Titles for the next six months...

January

THE VALTIERI MARRIAGE DEAL	Caroline Anderson
THE REBEL AND THE BABY DOCTOR	Joanna Neil
THE COUNTRY DOCTOR'S DAUGHTER	Gill Sanderson
SURGEON BOSS, BACHELOR DAD	Lucy Clark
THE GREEK DOCTOR'S PROPOSAL	Molly Evans
SINGLE FATHER: WIFE AND MOTHER WANTED	Sharon Archer

February

EMERGENCY: WIFE LOST AND FOUND	Carol Marinelli
A SPECIAL KIND OF FAMILY	Marion Lennox
HOT-SHOT SURGEON, CINDERELLA BRIDE	Alison Roberts
A SUMMER WEDDING AT WILLOWMERE	Abigail Gordon
MIRACLE: TWIN BABIES	Fiona Lowe
THE PLAYBOY DOCTOR CLAIMS HIS BRIDE	Janice Lynn

March

SECRET SHEIKH, SECRET BABY	Carol Marinelli
PREGNANT MIDWIFE: FATHER NEEDED	Fiona McArthur
HIS BABY BOMBSHELL	Jessica Matthews
FOUND: A MOTHER FOR HIS SON	Dianne Drake
THE PLAYBOY DOCTOR'S SURPRISE PROPOSAL	Anne Fraser
HIRED: GP AND WIFE	Judy Campbell

MEDICAL™

Large Print

April

ITALIAN DOCTOR, DREAM PROPOSAL	Margaret McDonagh
WANTED: A FATHER FOR HER TWINS	Emily Forbes
BRIDE ON THE CHILDREN'S WARD	Lucy Clark
MARRIAGE REUNITED: BABY ON THE WAY	Sharon Archer
THE REBEL OF PENHALLY BAY	Caroline Anderson
MARRYING THE PLAYBOY DOCTOR	Laura Iding

May

COUNTRY MIDWIFE, CHRISTMAS BRIDE	Abigail Gordon
GREEK DOCTOR: ONE MAGICAL CHRISTMAS	Meredith Webber
HER BABY OUT OF THE BLUE	Alison Roberts
A DOCTOR, A NURSE: A CHRISTMAS BABY	Amy Andrews
SPANISH DOCTOR, PREGNANT MIDWIFE	Anne Fraser
EXPECTING A CHRISTMAS MIRACLE	Laura Iding

June

SNOWBOUND: MIRACLE MARRIAGE	Sarah Morgan
CHRISTMAS EVE: DOORSTEP DELIVERY	Sarah Morgan
HOT-SHOT DOC, CHRISTMAS BRIDE	Joanna Neil
CHRISTMAS AT RIVERCUT MANOR	Gill Sanderson
FALLING FOR THE PLAYBOY MILLIONAIRE	Kate Hardy
THE SURGEON'S NEW-YEAR WEDDING WISH	Laura Iding

™ MILLS & BOON®

millsandboon.co.uk Community

Join Us!

he Community is the perfect place to meet and chat to kin-
red spirits who love books and reading as much as you do,
ut it's also the place to:

Get the inside scoop from authors about their latest books

Learn how to write a romance book with advice from our editors

Help us to continue publishing the best in women's fiction

Share your thoughts on the books we publish

Befriend other users

orums: Interact with each other as well as authors, editors
nd a whole host of other users worldwide.

Blogs: Every registered community member has their own
log to tell the world what they're up to and what's on their
nind.

Book Challenge: We're aiming to read 5,000 books and have
oined forces with The Reading Agency in our
naugural Book Challenge.

Profile Page: Showcase yourself and keep a record of your
ecent community activity.

Social Networking: We've added buttons at the end of every
ost to share via digg, Facebook, Google, Yahoo, technorati
nd de.licio.us.

www.millsandboon.co.uk